The Awakening of Jennifer Van Arsdale

"Political theorists often talk about the unintended consequences of liberal policies, but the abstract terms they use can't really summon up the untidy world of actual, ordinary people where those consequences cause one disaster after another. But George Leef's new novel takes us straight into that world and uncovers those unintended results as they appear seemingly from nowhere, scarring the lives of its people. The result is a political moral fable, but one set in the ordinary life of our time rather than in some nightmarish future like those of George Orwell and Aldous Huxley. It's as entertaining as it is instructive, and as an elucidation of political ideas it will probably be more effective than many a learned tract in political philosophy."

—Professor John Ellis, UC Santa Cruz

ꝏ

"Ideas have consequences and this engaging, readable novel brings to life the consequences of America continuing down the progressive policy path. *The Awakening of Jennifer Van Arsdale* is simply a great read as well as a crash course in some of the important policy debates of our time. It will lift the spirits of Americans who fear that we have gone past the point of no return."

—Carrie Lukas, President of Independent Women's Forum

༄

"This is an amusing tale of America on the wrong course, but potentially finding its way. Beneath the surface of George Leef's stock characters is a very human encounter with leftist arrogance and tyranny—precisely what we see on the rise in our country today, and which is steadily becoming a primary challenge in the ordinary lives of children in public schools, workers in their offices, and shoppers logging into Amazon. Have we had enough of it? Not yet, it seems. We have many arguments from scholars and commentators mounted against the progressivist wave, but they haven't slowed the momentum at all. Perhaps the greatest challenge to it will have to come from the creative side, from filmmakers and musicians and novelists. I predict that if you read this book you will find that Leef's fictional portrayal of hyper-leftist President Pat Farnsworth beats one thousand tweets complaining about the Biden Administration any day. And it's funny, too."

—Professor Mark Bauerlein, Emory University and editor, *First Things*

༄

"What would American life look like if the woke, statist, Constitution-shredding agenda of the Biden/Harris Democrats were fully enacted? George Leef answers that question with frightening plausibility, imagining a future that's barreling toward us like a train in a tunnel. Jennifer Van Arsdale is an Oberlin graduate and *Washington Post* reporter who sets aside her misgivings about the white patriarchy to indulge her love of concert performances of Bach and Beethoven. She is thrilled to be chosen as the official biographer of the first female president of the United States, a woman her political hit-pieces helped to elect on the platform 'The Nation That Cares.' But while visiting the former president's oceanfront estate, she runs into the real America, a wasteland of boarded-up storefronts and abandoned dreams that is the true legacy of progressivism. That's when her education—and the reader's—begins."

—Professor Jacob Howland, Tulsa University

℘

"George Leef delivers a fast-paced *Bildungsroman* recounting Jen Van Arsdale's journey from the Beltway swamp (her job at the *Washington Post*) to California's Third World landscape of pustulating tarp cities, open air privies, shredded freedoms, and shattered monuments.

"Jen's guides to enlightenment are a series of regular Americans who explain not just what happened in the Left Coast one-party state, but how and why: how education became indoctrination, how journalism mutated into propaganda, how the economy was crippled by regulation and boondoggles, and why history and beauty now reside in the dumpster.

"How will Jen respond and what is the one touchstone that sustains her? The *L.A. Times* brags that California is 'The State of What's Next.' Oh no! What a timely novel...and warning."

—Professor David Clemens, Monterey Peninsula College

The Awakening of Jennifer Van Arsdale

A POLITICAL FABLE FOR OUR TIME

GEORGE C. LEEF

Published by Bombardier Books
An Imprint of Post Hill Press
ISBN: 978-1-63758-356-2
ISBN (eBook): 978-1-63758-357-9

The Awakening of Jennifer Van Arsdale:
A Political Fable For Our Time
© 2022 by George C. Leef
All Rights Reserved

Cover Design by Tiffani Shea

This book is a work of fiction. People, places, events, and situations are the product of the author's imagination. Any resemblance to actual persons, living or dead, or historical events, is purely coincidental.

No part of this book may be reproduced, stored in a retrieval system, or transmitted by any means without the written permission of the author and publisher.

Post Hill Press
New York • Nashville
posthillpress.com

Published in the United States of America
1 2 3 4 5 6 7 8 9 10

For Ann

TABLE OF CONTENTS

CHAPTER 1

A Glorious Day in May

The first rays of light filtered into Jennifer Van Arsdale's bedroom, and that was all it ever took to wake her up. She opened her eyes and looked at the clock on the nightstand: 5:42 a.m. She stretched and got out of bed.

Jen walked downstairs into the stylish kitchen of her townhouse on a shady street in the northwest corner of the District of Columbia. She had had the place remodeled just a few months earlier and was delighted with the new cabinets, appliances, and highest-grade granite countertops.

The new kitchen was particularly spectacular, she thought, but the renovation had been much more expensive than imagined, consuming nearly all of her savings. Prices for everything had been rising rapidly for several years.

"Yes, I know it's a lot, Ms. Van Arsdale," her designer had said, a tad apologetically, "but with the cost increases we are expecting, this job will be at least fifteen to twenty percent higher next year."

When the designer had shown her the final cost figure, Jen had actually gasped. "Why can't the government control inflation?" she replied with a sigh. Fortunately, her job at the *Washington Post* was secure and paid well. Still, a big raise this year would help. She resolved to do her utmost to impress the newspaper's management.

Jen started the Nespresso, took a bunch of organic red grapes from the fridge, then sat down at her new kitchen table. She opened her laptop, going immediately to *washingtonpost.com*. The news was not good. The lead stories covered rising tension in the Middle East, a bad spring cold snap that was going to lower agricultural production, and a big fall in the stock market. She took a grape and switched over to the editorial page.

"The Government Must Act to Slow Inflation," read the lead editorial. Jen knew the trio that had written it and was quite sure what it would say, but she read it anyway.

> *The new administration has yet to show the determination that is essential if the country is to get a handle on the rapid increase in prices. Inflation had gathered strength throughout President Patricia Farnsworth's two terms, but her efforts at slowing it were not effective. President Frances Barlow has been in the White House for almost four months and her pronouncements on the evils of inflation are no better than Gerald Ford's 'Whip Inflation Now' buttons back in 1975. If Barlow doesn't take this problem more seriously, she will help elevate Conservative Republican candidates who will capitalize on the public anger at soaring prices. Leading economists are pointing out that strict federal controls kept inflation down during World War II. Perhaps it is time to look at that experience.*

Jen agreed. The Nespresso beeped. She poured a large mug and sat back. Allegro, her Turkish Angora cat strolled over and rubbed her ankle. Jen reached down and stroked her head.

While sipping the hot coffee, Jen went to her email.

The first message sent the night before was from her editor at the *Post*, Gabrielle Tartakover.

"Hi, Jen. Just a reminder that I need—by this evening—that article about remaining conservative professors and their corrupting influence on students. And how about punching up your lede. Let's get the word 'hate' in there to get more attention."

"I have the piece nearly ready, Gabrielle," Jen typed. "I'll revise it and send it this afternoon. You're right that attracting readers is the key." She hit "Send."

The subject of the article was specifically college professors who disagreed with progressivism—those who oppose wealth redistribution, minimum wage laws, reparations, and single-payer health care—and those who *still* argue that human sexuality is binary and that climate change is not a looming disaster. Professors who said such things were unfit to teach American students, and exposing them to ridicule was a job that Jen relished. She would have the piece finished in just a few hours. After that, she'd have several hours to research her next book on the visionary college presidents who had helped transform American higher education.

Jen decided that she'd do her daily Peloton ride first. Keeping fit was always a top priority for her. At forty-four, she was as trim as she'd been at twenty-four.

Taking a few more grapes, Jen thought ahead to the evening. She had a ticket for a piano recital by a young Swiss virtuoso, Wilhelm Steinbacher, who would be playing Bach, Beethoven, and Liszt at the John F. Kennedy Center, overlooking the Potomac River across from swanky Georgetown.

Jen had loved classical music since she was very young. That was a gift from her grandmother who began teaching her to play the piano at the age of three, and took her to concerts in Grand Rapids, Michigan where she first heard works by the famous composers. Steinbacher had been getting outstanding reviews in Europe. She was eager to hear him perform live.

The ticket had cost $250—and for a seat that wasn't even very good. Jen could remember when concert tickets had cost less than half that. Of course, the Kennedy Center was facing rising expenses and had to increase ticket prices accordingly.

However, the ticket price was a minor matter compared to the hazard involved with attending classical concerts these days.

A number of prominent social commentators had declared that classical music was "problematic" due to its "white male dominance." Attending a concert that featured a white male soloist and music by three white men could lead to trouble. If Jen were seen there, someone might criticize her for supporting the "white male power structure" that was at the root of nearly all the world's troubles.

Jen simply loved the music and didn't agree that it had anything to do with the world's troubles. But she knew that there was no point in arguing with the activists once they had decided to go after you for a violation of their values. Good people had had their careers damaged for lesser political missteps, and Jen didn't want to put hers in jeopardy. She knew that she had to be very careful.

In defense, Jen had developed a set of precautions for certain concerts. She would wear unobtrusive clothing, arrive very early to pick up the ticket (always ordered by her sister, Madeleine White, and under her name.) Then she would sit with her head down, looking at her iPhone until the program began. She never looked around—to avoid the possibility of eye contact—and lingered unobtrusively afterwards to minimize the chances of being noticed on the way out.

It helped that Jen was short and slight. Wearing an ordinary coat and a large hat, she was as inconspicuous as possible.

Living in Washington had its dangers. Street-smart people could largely protect themselves from the obvious ones: the increasing number of break-ins, assaults, and dangerously aggressive panhandlers. But it was becoming much harder to protect against the omnipresent mobile devices and Twitter mobs. A mere accusation could instantly cause an avalanche of outrage, real or feigned, that usually proved ruinous to lives and careers. Jen just loved music too much to give up concerts completely. She just had to be careful.

Early in the afternoon, Jen took a break and called her friend, Samantha Swan, the *Post's* restaurant critic.

"Feel like an early dinner, Sam? I need to be done by seven, though. If you're free, pick a nice place in town."

"That sounds good. There's a new French restaurant on L Street that's terrific—*Blanchisserie Francais*. It's simply *to die for*, Jen. On a Friday night, it's probably already booked solid, but I'm sure I can get us an early table. I'll make the reservation and text you the address."

Jen arrived at the restaurant first and told the *maître d'* that she was waiting for Samantha Swan. He beamed and said, with what Jen thought was a put-on French accent, "Ah, Mademoiselle Swan. She is a very good friend of this restaurant!"

At that moment, Sam walked in. She was a stylish woman of fifty-three who had befriended Jen right after the *Post* hired her. Sam was good company, except for her need to remind everyone that she had a degree in art history from Yale.

"Welcome, my dear Sam! How delightful to see you again," said the maître *d'*. "I have a very nice table for you and Mademoiselle Van Arsdale. Please follow me."

Once they were seated, Jen said to Sam, "You're certainly popular here."

"That's true, I gave *Blanchisserie Francois* a glowing review right after it opened in March. The owners know how much that meant to their success. They'll happily comp the check tonight, so don't give a thought to the stratospheric prices."

The waiter arrived at their table with the menus. Jen really was shocked at the prices, though she almost never dined at top-tier restaurants.

After the two ordered, Jen asked, "How are you doing these days? I take it that there is still a lot for you to write about on the city's restaurant scene."

Sam grimaced slightly.

"It's harder than it used to be. There just aren't as many restaurants. Quite a few that closed during Covid never reopened, and some that did couldn't survive with the higher cost of help. I'm finding it more difficult to come up with columns about the food scene. Some other big city outlets have entirely dumped their restaurant critics. I'm doing my best to make sure the *Post* doesn't find me expendable."

Jen knew that Sam and her husband were loaded. He was a trust fund baby who showered money on a wide array of progressive causes and candidates. To them, Sam's check from the *Post* was loose change. For Sam, the prestige of writing her restaurant column was the main thing.

"I sure hope the paper keeps you. How else would the elite know where to dine?" Jen joked.

Sam laughed, buttered a roll, then asked, "And how about you? I shouldn't think you'd have anything to worry about, especially since you were nominated for a Pulitzer last year, right?"

"Thanks for mentioning that. I wish I'd won. I still can't believe the prize went to Charles Chesterton. Did you hear the feature with the *LA Times* that got him the award was based on made-up interviews? And yet he gets to keep it. The Pulitzer Committee said something banal like, 'Chesterton may have fabricated some of his material, but his work speaks to deep truths that cannot be ignored.' Maybe I'll have another shot this year."

Sam gestured with the roll in her hand, saying, "Jen, you're *much better* than he is and you don't make stuff up. You'll have a good chance this time around. What are you working on now?"

"Well, just this afternoon I sent off my next column to Gabrielle. It's about right-wing professors who keep saying and writing indefensible things. At her suggestion, my lede is about the 'voices of hate that still resound on campus.' I think 'hate' is too strong a word, but she knows what will grab readers."

Sam snorted.

"Jen, your only problem is that you can be too nice. Those Neanderthals with their backward ideas need to be exposed and silenced, permanently. I'm just a little surprised there are any left."

Buttering her roll, Jen replied, "Well, there are a few. Fortunately, many students are tireless in reporting on faculty members who say hurtful things about affirmative action programs or gender identity. Their statements get reported to Bias Incident Response Teams. They made it was easy for me to write my article."

"I look forward to reading it. Working on anything else?"

The waiter brought Jen and Sam their bouillabaisse. After he had gone, Jen replied, "I have a book deal. It's about the visionary college and university presidents who have done so much to revolutionize higher education." She chuckled, "It won't make me rich, but it might at least pay for my kitchen remodeling."

Jen and Sam finished dinner right at 7:00 p.m. As they were leaving, Sam asked, "So where are you off to this evening? Why the hurry?"

Good a friend as Sam was, Jen didn't want to tell her the truth. Thinking fast, she replied, "I'm babysitting my niece this evening, so my sister and her husband can go to a concert."

"There you go again, Jen—being nice," said Sam as she got into her taxi.

A minute later, Jen hailed a taxi for the ride to the Kennedy Center. She was the only person in the will-call line when it opened.

"A ticket for Madeleine White, please," she said to the attendant, keeping her eyes down.

Ticket in hand, Jen walked into the empty hall. An usher asked if she needed help finding her seat, but she demurred. Jen knew the exact location. For career safety reasons, she had chosen an aisle seat on the left side near the back. She felt that it was least likely that anyone would happen to notice her there.

The concert wouldn't begin for more than half an hour. Jen checked her iPhone for email before putting it on silent. Then she buried her face in the program, never looking up, even as people moved past her to get to their seats. Eye contact had to be avoided.

Precisely at 8:00 p.m., Wilhelm Steinbacher strode out on stage. Jen wondered if his playing would live up to the reviews.

Steinbacher began with Ferruccio Busoni's transcription of Bach's great *Chaconne* for solo violin. He followed that stupendous work with Beethoven's *Appassionata* Sonata; his playing was powerful, precise, and exciting. Jen was loving the evening.

During the intermission, she remained in her seat, her face, she hoped, obscured by the program. People sidled by her, but she never looked up. After the intermission was over, Jen heard the woman seated to her right say, "Greg, let's take a selfie for the kids." When she heard those words, she turned away to minimize the chances that she might be recognized in the couple's photo. She was irked. Now there was a tiny reason for concern.

After the intermission, Steinbacher played Liszt's *Transcendental Etudes*. His playing throughout those twelve tremendous pieces was electrifying.

After the final chord of the last etude, the audience cheered Steinbacher, calling the young virtuoso back to the stage six times before he sat down again to play one of Chopin's waltzes as an encore.

What a fabulous night of music, Jen thought after the applause ended. *Now be careful getting home.*

She lingered in the back of the hall, pretending to read the program notes until the audience had filed out and it was safe to get a taxi.

Within ten minutes, Jen was back in her townhouse. Allegro was asleep on the sofa.

Jen hung up her coat then checked her phone. She saw that a voice message had been left during the concert. It was a local Washington "202" number, and the caller was "CJOliver." Jen was ready to call it a day, but she was too curious. She clicked.

"Hello Ms. Van Arsdale, this is Courtney J. Oliver. I'm the Chief of Staff to former President Patricia Farnsworth. She is looking for an excellent writer to do an authorized biography. You are among those under consideration. The compensation would be substantial. I have also sent you an email about this opportunity. Please either reply to it or call me back at your earliest convenience. Thank you."

Jen was now exhausted but couldn't wait to respond. She tapped his number and held her breath.

"Hello, Ms. Van Arsdale. Thank you for returning my call so promptly," said a man's voice with a Boston accent.

"Sorry I missed your call, Mr. Oliver. I was out at a concert this evening. When I heard your message, I wanted to speak with you without delay."

"I know it's a bit late on the East Coast," Courtney replied, "but this won't take very long. As I said, President Farnsworth is looking for a top-notch writer to take on a task she regards as supremely important—her biography...her legacy. Several of us who are close to her have compiled a list of prospective writers and you are one of them. I just want to find out whether you would like to stay on our list as we move forward."

Trying not to sound overly eager, Jen replied, "Yes, I certainly do want to stay on your list. Writing the authorized biography of our first woman president would be a project I would relish."

"Splendid, Ms. Van Arsdale. President Farnsworth would like to initially speak with each of the people we are considering over the phone tomorrow. Could you do around noon?"

"Yes, I will look forward to it."

"Very good. I will call you tomorrow. Thank you and have a good evening."

Jen sank down onto her sofa and looked at the ceiling as she thought about having a chance to write the biography of America's first woman president—by almost all accounts, the nation's greatest political leader since Franklin D. Roosevelt.

Pat Farnsworth had united the country, virtually eliminated unemployment, ensured medical care for all, and ended America's addiction to fossil fuels, among many other great accomplishments. For any president to have so transformed the country, putting equality, safety, and social justice ahead of the nation's old obsessions with money and profit and founding principles was amazing. And that it was a *woman* who had done it was truly something to savor.

And now she, Jennifer Van Arsdale from little Vriesland, Michigan, might be her biographer. Writing that book would be a labor of love—if she got the chance. *And it all could be decided tomorrow.*

Jen was now too keyed up to sleep. She opened her MacBook Pro to check out the news on the *Post's* site. Finding none, she scrolled down to the arts section and was surprised to see that a review of the Steinbacher concert was already up.

The review had been written by Amanda Putnam-Rovere. Jen winced. The paper was grooming her to replace its octogenarian music critic, Albert Redenius. He was immensely knowledgeable about music and wrote superb reviews. Unfortunately, he was so antiquated that he refused to go along with gender-neutral writing conventions and the new fashion of bringing politics into music reviews. Albert had even dared defend the idea that auditions for the orchestra should be blind and based on pure talent, rather than by prioritizing each musician's ethnicity to achieve an "inclusive" and "diverse" ensemble. Jen agreed with him, but could never say so.

Jen began to read Amanda's review.

"On Friday evening, Swiss pianist Wilhelm Steinbacher played a recital at the Kennedy Center. Before going into the details of Herr Steinbacher's performance, a question simply must be asked: Why does the management of the Center continue scheduling concerts that are utterly lacking in diversity? Here we had a white male pianist playing music by three white male composers.

"Evidently, the Center's managers do not grasp what a message of despair it sends to women and Black, Indigenous, and People of Color when they have programs such as tonight's. Are they invisible? Don't they matter? This reviewer says that it's time for the Kennedy Center to stop supporting white male hegemony."

Jen had already read enough.

Had Amanda even been there to see that quite a few women and people of color had *loved* Steinbacher's concert? Why couldn't critics of music—or anything else—stick to the subject without wandering off-topic to talk about their political commitments? Were the paper's editors afraid to tell such writers that not *everything* had to be about politics?

Apparently, they were, judging from the increasing number of young writers who knew little about their subjects, but were exceedingly proficient at filling up columns with important-sounding yet empty jargon learned as liberal arts undergrads.

Sure, Jen was all for social change. America still needed much more of it, even after the historic presidency of Pat Farnsworth. She appreciated the dedication of young people like Amanda to the cause. But couldn't they see when they were going too far? Why did they have to let ideology get in the way of objectivity and fairness?

Yes, the world of classical music was largely white, but all that people really cared about was *the music*. If you could play well enough, nobody cared about anything else about you.

You close your eyes and listen. As for composers, the ones who were most popular had achieved their rank because they connected listeners most deeply with the music, not because of their race or sexual identity.

In America, it was possible to fake many things. You could pretend to be an artist by splashing paint on a canvas. You could pretend to be a writer by producing word salads. But to *compose* great music took real talent. No one had come along with enough of that to shoulder aside Bach, Beethoven, and Liszt.

If young people like Amanda Putnam-Rovere got their way and forced classical music to be "equitable," music lovers would suffer. And America wouldn't be the slightest bit better, either.

Nevertheless, the review served as a strong reminder to Jen that she needed to be careful. Imagine what would happen if Amanda or one of her clones around the city were to put up a Facebook post with Jen's photo and the caption, "Why does 'progressive' writer Jennifer Van Arsdale patronize and endorse concerts that perpetuate white privilege?"

Jen closed her computer and went upstairs to bed.

CHAPTER 2

The Book Deal

Jen woke up at 5:41 a.m. It was Saturday morning. Immediately, she remembered the previous night's call from Courtney Oliver and the upcoming call with President Farnsworth at noon. Her heart rate quickened.

Allegro was on the end of her bed, staring at her. Jen stroked her lustrous coat and said, "This could be a big day for us, my little friend."

She got busy with her normal routine, but glanced at the clock time and again. The 11:00 a.m. hour seemed to drag by interminably. Jen tried rehearsing what she'd say to the former president that might work in her favor.

She checked her phone to be sure it was fully charged.

At noon, she was cleaning her already spotless kitchen, wondering when her phone would ring. She was staring at it when, at 12:02, the call came in.

"Good morning, Mr. Oliver."

"And a good morning to you, Ms. Van Arsdale. I will have President Farnsworth on the line in a minute. Let me first say that she admires your writing and regards you as a strong ally in the struggle to remake the nation. She told me that she thinks one of the articles you wrote during her first campaign was instrumental in exposing the ugly hidden agenda of her opponent. His polling never recovered after it ran."

"Oh, you mean the piece on his plan to use the Department of Education to require the teaching of creationism in public schools?" Jen replied. "I considered that my own 'October Surprise.' There was barely a smidgen of truth in it, but it certainly energized the president's base."

The smidgen of truth, of course, came from "unnamed sources," reinforced by red-hot denunciations from activist professors and the education lobby. The "Creationist Plot" was entirely Jen's concoction, and it had worked beautifully. She had written quite a few political attack pieces, but that one made her the proudest. That Pat Farnsworth remembered it was a good sign.

"Oh, that piece was a stroke of genius," Courtney replied. He paused, then said, "I see that the president is just finishing up on another call. She will be with you soon."

Jen wasn't sure how to respond, though felt the need to fill the time until Pat Farnsworth was ready to speak.

"So, I understand that President Farnsworth has retired back home to California, is that right?"

"Yes, I'm calling from her home near Laguna Beach."

"Could I ask a few quick questions about the biography you have in mind?"

"Naturally, Ms. Van Arsdale."

"All right. What about the timeline? How quickly would you want the book?"

"We would like a draft within six months."

"I'm sure I could do that. And do you have a publisher lined up?"

"Yes, we have that arranged. It is obviously one of the country's most prestigious."

"As I had expected. And what about the President's compensation?"

"The author will receive a four-million-dollar advance. And with the royalties on what we are sure will be a massive bestseller, the book will be worth several times that."

Jen paused a moment to try to think about that sum. If she got the job, it would eliminate her money concerns forever.

Attempting to control her enthusiasm, Jen responded, "And how about access to the President and her papers?"

"The President would fly you out to California in a private plane for several days of intensive interviews, and, of course, we'd make any documents you think pertinent available to you."

Before Jen could reply, Courtney said, "President Farnsworth is now ready to speak with you, Ms. Van Arsdale. I'm going to transfer you over to her."

Jen felt a surge of adrenaline. She held her breath and then in a moment, she heard the familiar, somewhat gruff sound of Pat Farnsworth's voice.

"Hello, Ms. Van Arsdale. This is Pat Farnsworth. I'm so happy to speak with you."

"It's my honor, Madam President. I have always been a great supporter of yours."

"Yes, I know that very well. That's why you are one of the final two people I am considering for my biography. You're an excellent writer, and deeply committed to the same goals I am: social justice, equity, and the healing of America's old wounds. Have you had time to think about the approach you would take if we were to work together?"

Jen had indeed anticipated such a question and rehearsed an answer.

"First, thanks for your kind words, Madam President. As for the biography, I think that the crucial thing would be to trace the chord of your philosophy of life and government from your school days through your entire political career. I would drive home to the readers that you have been a steadfast advocate for the transformation of America, willing to take on all opponents to bring that about."

"Good, good. Please go on."

"I would also want readers to understand the obstacles you had to overcome to become our first woman president, especially the men who thought you weren't tough enough. I would also devote a significant part of the book to how you won the country over *intellectually*, presenting the case for progressive policies so convincingly that the opposition was defeated once and for all."

"I like the sound of that. Make the book as much about the war of ideas I waged as much as a recounting of my life. I don't mind letting you know that I would like the American people to see me as a serious thinker as much as a successful politician."

Pat paused a second and then asked, "Has Mr. Oliver explained that we would want a draft within six months? Would that be any problem for you?"

"No, it wouldn't," Jen replied with emphasis. "I'm currently working on another book, but I would put that project on hold. As for the *Post*, my editor doesn't care what else I do as long as I write my regular columns on time. Plus, this book would be a boon to the paper."

"And if we choose you, when would you be free to fly out to California for several days of interviews next week?"

"I could leave at any time, Madam President. I'm eager to get started."

Jen hoped that she was showing just the right amount of enthusiasm.

"Fine. We are on the cusp of our decision, Ms. Van Arsdale. Mr. Oliver will get back to you soon. Good bye."

"Good bye, Madam President."

How soon would "soon" be, Jen wondered.

The call with the former President left Jen feeling very upbeat and she wanted some music to match her mood. She thought a moment and realized that the perfect piece would be Beethoven's sprightly Eighth. She put on Spotify and busied herself with little household tasks. She knew she wouldn't be able to concentrate on serious work until she knew whether or not she'd be chosen to write the biography.

Just as the symphony's finale was beginning, Jen's phone rang. She could see that it was Courtney Oliver. Her pulse quickened.

"Hello, Mr. Oliver."

"Hello again, Ms. Van Arsdale. I have good news for you. The President has made her decision—she wants *you* to write her biography."

Jen took a moment to compose herself.

"Oh, thank you so much, Mr. Oliver. That's just fantastic. I can hardly wait to get started."

"Well, you won't have to wait long. President Farnsworth would like to begin this coming Tuesday, since she will be leaving a week after that for a vacation in the Seychelles. I will clear her schedule from Tuesday through Friday. I will also arrange for car service to pick you up at your home at around 7:00 a.m. on Tuesday. You'll be driven to the private hangar area at Dulles Airport and met by our representative. I will arrange for a private jet to fly you to Orange County Airport. There, you will be met by the President's chauffeur and driven to her home—*Vista del Oceano*. I will make the arrangements with the car service in DC and text them to you. I will also reserve a suite for you at the Ritz-Carlton at Dana Point, which is quite close to the President's home."

"Thank you so much, Mr. Oliver. That all sounds fantastic."

"I have no doubt that President Farnsworth has made the best choice, Ms. Van Arsdale. I will see you on Tuesday. Enjoy the rest of your weekend."

"I'm looking forward to it, Mr. Oliver."

Jen simply had to tell people about this news, and the first person to call was her kid sister.

"Hi, Maddy. Got a minute to talk? I have got to tell you this. I have a new book contract. I'm going to write President Farnsworth's authorized biography. She wants *me* to do it. The book deal will be worth millions!"

Jen heard Maddy take a long breath. They didn't agree on politics, and Maddy was probably thinking up a sharp retort.

"Well, that's terrific, Jen. I'm glad you'll be able to cash in, writing about someone you find so admirable. Maybe you'll be able to spend the money before it loses all its value."

There it was. But Jen wasn't going to let her little sister's backward political ideas dampen her mood.

"Aw come on, Maddy. Things aren't so bad in the country. Your music business is pretty good, isn't it? Admit it, you're at least a bit proud of our first female president, aren't you?"

"No, Jen. I think Pat Farnsworth pushed the country to the brink of economic disaster and Franny Barlow is going to take us over the edge. But still, I'm glad you're going to have this opportunity."

"And I'm glad to hear you say that, Maddy. They're going to fly me out to meet with President Farnsworth on Tuesday morning. I will have several days of interviews with her. Then I'll dive into the writing. They want the manuscript in six months."

"That sounds like just your cup of tea. I'm sure you'll do a superb job on the biography. And hey, if our music store needs some capital, could I borrow a few million from you?" her sister joked.

"Yeah, sure. I'll talk to you again soon, Maddy."

Jen began making a list of things for the trip to California. It was the same way she used to feel on Christmas Eve when she was little.

CHAPTER 3

Getting to Know POTUS

Tuesday morning was unseasonably cool as a black SUV pulled up in front of Jen's townhouse. The driver had texted her to expect him at 7:05 a.m. Jen was ready, having already been awake for two hours. Everything she would need was at the front door: her suitcase, large purse, jacket, and hat.

Jen had filled Allegro's food and water station. When she saw a vehicle pull up in front of her house, she picked up the little cat and said, "You'll have the mind the store for a few days while I'm gone, okay?"

The doorbell rang and Jen opened it to see a middle-aged man wearing a rather worn gray suit.

"Good morning, Ms. Van Arsdale. I'm Spiros, and I'll be driving you to Dulles Airport."

He picked up Jen's suitcase. She locked the door, and they walked to the waiting vehicle. Spiros helped Jen in, tucked her suitcase in the back, cranked the engine, and edged delicately into traffic. Jen wondered if this was the beginning of something great—an odyssey of sorts.

Lost in thought, Jen was surprised to see they were already turning off the toll road to go to Dulles Airport. Spiros drove to a part of the airport she had never seen before, the area where private planes were kept.

A young woman in a stylish blue uniform approached the SUV. Once Spiros had opened the door, she said, "Good morning, Ms. Van Arsdale. I will get you boarded, and we'll be on our way to California." She wore a name tag reading "Sally Judkins," so Jen said, "Thank you very much, Sally."

Jen boarded the plane and looked around the luxurious cabin. It could seat eight, but she was the only passenger. Sally asked her to choose a seat. Jen did so, buckled in, and the plane began to taxi within a minute.

As the jet ascended, Jen watched the green hills of Northern Virginia beneath her for ten minutes and then fell fast asleep.

When she woke up, she looked out the window and saw a brownish landscape she assumed was New Mexico or Arizona. Sally Judkins walked over to her.

"We'll be landing in about an hour and a half, Ms. Van Arsdale. What can I get for you? Champagne? Fresh fruit? Eggs. Just name it."

"Thank you. I'd like a glass of orange juice and an omelet with gruyere cheese, mushrooms, and green pepper, if that's possible."

"Absolutely. I'll have your juice for you in a moment, and your omelet will be ready in a few minutes."

Jen looked out the window and thought that she would enjoy this sort of luxury all the time once she began cashing in on her biography of Pat Farnsworth.

She enjoyed her meal then sat back to think about the days ahead.

After the plane landed, Sally escorted Jen into a hangar at Orange County Airport, where a rough-looking man in a black suit was waiting.

"Welcome, Ms. Van Arsdale. I'm Jurgen, President Farnsworth's driver. I have our vehicle ready to take you to her home in Laguna Beach."

"Very good, Jurgen. I'm eager to meet the President."

Jurgen placed Jen's suitcase in the back of the vehicle while Jen carried her purse and hat. As they drove out of the airport, Jen saw the famous California palm trees and bright sun. With her light skin, she would certainly need her hat and sunscreen if she were outside for any length of time.

After a drive of fifteen minutes or so, the vehicle stopped at a foreboding gate. Jen could see security cameras pointing along a high black metal fence. A former President of the United States would still have nothing less than top-flight security. The gate slowly opened, and Jurgen drove up the winding driveway.

The vehicle stopped on the circular drive in front of the President's house. Through the dark glass, Jen could see a tall, white-haired man in a dark suit walk up and open the door for her.

"Welcome to *Vista del Oceano*, Ms. Van Arsdale. I'm Courtney Oliver. Was everything satisfactory on your trip?"

"So nice to meet you, Mr. Oliver, and yes, my trip couldn't have been better. I'm excited to be here. The President's home is spectacular."

"It certainly is. Let's go in and meet the President."

Jen followed Courtney to the ornate front doors, which appeared to be made of some exotic reddish wood, perhaps cocobolo. Courtney opened the right of the two panels and beckoned Jen into a huge room with windows that must have been at least twelve feet high, looking out onto the Pacific. Jen had never seen a room so magnificent.

She gazed around, trying to focus her mind on the day ahead, her first interview with the woman who had brought such dramatic change to the country over the last eight years. Pat Farnsworth had transformed the United States from a nation without a conscience into, as her campaign theme said, "The Nation that Cares."

Thanks to her two terms in the White House, America had turned a corner, leaving behind its ugly past and moving forward into fairness, justice, and safety for all people. She had routed the forces that sought to preserve their so-called constitutional rights. And now she, Jennifer Van Arsdale, was about to begin the process of writing the biography of America's first woman president and undoubtedly the best president of all.

Staring around the room and dumbstruck by the events of the last three days, Jen struggled to come up with something intelligent to say to Courtney when a motion caught her eye. President Farnsworth had entered the room.

Farnsworth was of medium height with striking facial features—large, rather bulging blue eyes, a prominent nose, and a small, pursed mouth that gave her a severe visage. Political cartoonists always exaggerated them in their caricatures. Her gray hair was stylishly cut. She wore a light blue blouse with dark blue casual pants.

Courtney spoke, "Ms. Van Arsdale, meet President Farnsworth."

"Jennifer Van Arsdale," the former President began in her familiar, loud voice, "I am *so pleased* to meet you."

Beaming, Jen replied, "Madam President, this is a great honor. I can't begin to say how thrilled I am to have this opportunity, to meet with you and to write about your remarkable life. And I must say that your home is *spectacular*."

The President made a broad, sweeping motion with her arm. "We call it *Vista del Oceano*," she said, giving each word grand emphasis.

"Let's put this on a first name basis right away. Call me Pat, please."

"Certainly, Pat. And I prefer Jen."

"Very good, Jen. How about if we go out onto the veranda to talk?"

"It is delightful to have met you, Ms. Van Arsdale," said Courtney as he turned and walked away.

Pat motioned and led Jen out to a *breathtaking* veranda. That much-overworked word from the world of real estate actually applied here. Jen's eyes were dazzled by the flowers in cobalt blue ceramic planters, the palm trees, the swimming pool with its edging of colorful tile. Pat led the way to a glass-topped table and chairs under a striped awning.

"Let's talk here, Jen. How about some iced tea? Or something stronger if you'd like."

"Iced tea would be just right, thank you."

Jen took a deep breath.

"Pat, I can't even begin to tell you how much I admire you for all you have done to make America a decent, caring nation. Writing your biography will be a labor of love."

"I greatly appreciate your kind words, Jen. Ever since I entered politics, I've been striving to turn America into exactly the kind of nation it always should have been—one where everyone is safe, where everyone is free from hatred and violence, where everyone is equal and feels respected. I truly believe that we have put the country on the right path, and that it will never turn back."

Jen nodded vigorously. She knew those lines, for they were from Pat's final State of the Union address. They were incontestably true. *The country will never turn back.*

"Shall we start, Pat? All right if I record our sessions?"

"Oh, certainly."

Jen opened her notebook filled with questions she had prepared.

"I would like to begin with your childhood. Please tell me anything you think that readers would want to know about your family and early years."

Pat smiled and leaned back in her chair.

"I was born into a successful business family in Connecticut. My grandfather started a dry-cleaning company in Hartford. It grew, and as it did, he branched out into residential real estate—apartments for the middle class. In time, my father took the reins of those business ventures and turned them into two of the biggest in the state. I often heard him say that he was putting most of his profits into expansion. That must have been a good decision since we lived quite well. I was an only child, and my folks gave me everything a girl could want. When I was twelve, I said that I wanted riding lessons for my birthday, and they went ahead and got me a beautiful horse that I named Chester.

"I'd have to say that my schooling was pretty uneventful until high school. I took a couple of terrific courses in my junior year, courses that completely changed my outlook on life."

"Was it a public or a private high school, Pat?"

"It was private. My dad was very much a libertarian and I sometimes heard him say that he wished we could have a separation of school and state. For some reason, he thought that education should be completely voluntary. Besides his philosophy, the private schools were more prestigious and safer, so that settled it."

"Okay. Now I'm eager to hear about those courses you mentioned."

Pat leaned forward in her chair.

"The first one was Economics. The teacher, Mr. Prohaska, showed us how a capitalistic economy was unstable and unfair. Unstable because it necessarily goes through repeated boom and bust cycles that can only be controlled by government policies. The economy, we learned, was like a machine that often either overheated or sputtered down on its own, so we need wise federal control to keep it tuned and running well.

"And we learned that capitalism was unfair because workers are underpaid and consumers are overcharged by greedy business owners. The solution to that, he taught, was either to have widespread government regulation of business to ensure that wages and prices were fair, which some experts called for, or complete socialism, as others favored. I got an A on my term paper, 'Why America Must Try Socialism.'"

At that, Jen chuckled as she took a sip of iced tea. "And how did your businessman father like that?"

"Well, I never brought up such controversial things with him. He and my mom only knew I was getting straight A's, and they didn't nose into any of the details. I was in an award-winning school with a faculty full of teachers with great credentials. That was good enough for them.

"Basically, my parents were good people, but their beliefs were so antiquated. I'm sure they never meant anyone harm. They just couldn't see that what I often heard my dad call 'the spontaneous order of a free society' was a recipe for chaos and inequity. Nor did he get that his profits were money he had unfairly squeezed out of society. Mom and dad didn't have any idea that a revolutionary was living under their roof!

"If they were still alive, I think they'd recognize that our new America, under enlightened control, is so much better—more just and progressive—than the old America they grew up in."

Jen nodded at Pat and said, "Yes, of course they would. Now, what about the second course you mentioned?"

"Sure. That was U.S. History. It was taught by Ms. Armour. She emphasized that America had a dark, shameful history rather than one to celebrate. It was marked by the stealing of land from Native Americans, slavery, exploitation of immigrants, oppression of women—you know."

Jen nodded vigorously. "Of course."

"Ms. Armour sparked my activism. I came to understand that our institutions were basically unfair, meant to prop up elite white male property owners at the expense of everyone else. The nation could never achieve its promise until those institutions were replaced. Replacing them would require dedicated change agents like herself. She often said 'If you're not part of the solution, you're part of the problem.' Naturally, my friends and I wanted to be part of the solution. There was one kid who kept annoying everyone with questions like, 'Didn't our original institutions enable a lot of people to prosper?' and 'What if the new institutions make things worse?' Ms. Armour's reply was always, 'Mr. Stern, asking that question only proves that you're happy to be part of the problem.' Finally, he just shut up.

"Now, the solution, Ms. Amour said, was to change the government so that ordinary people would finally have control. 'A true democracy to replace our plutocracy' was another of her sayings. We needed income redistribution, but above all *power redistribution* so the marginalized would finally get their fair share of the nation's wealth.

"I'll never forget the charts she showed on the enormous disparities between the haves and have nots, despite our so-called welfare system. How the rich kept getting richer and the poor getting poorer. We spent a lot class of time discussing how to bring about the changes America needed."

"Your family was definitely among the haves, weren't they?" Jen asked.

"Absolutely, and I felt very guilty about it. I realized that my family was complicit in America's cancerous history. No doubt the workers in our companies were underpaid and overworked. No doubt the rents for our apartments were too high. I didn't really see my parents and grandparents as 'evil people,' but I knew that they were part of an *evil system*. That system had to be destroyed and replaced with humane institutions."

"I imagine that you never discussed Ms. Armour's class with your parents either."

"No, of course not. I'm sure my dad would have had a bunch of counter-arguments, but I didn't want him to sway me. Becoming an activist for social justice just felt so good, so right."

"Naturally. Now, did you have any extra-curricular activities in high school?"

"I did. I was in debate. My partner and I won far more debates than we lost. We had a shot at the Connecticut State Championship as seniors, but an incompetent fool of a judge gave us a loss in the semi-final round. My rebuttal demolished the Negative team's case, but somehow he managed to miss it."

Pat's tone had become angry. She stopped for a long drink of iced tea.

"That must have been hard to take.

"It sure was. The topic was 'Resolved that the United States should adopt a universal basic income policy' and our case was rock solid. Impregnable. I think that judge must have been some kind of conservative hard-liner who just couldn't stand to hear such a potent attack on his beliefs."

"Yeah, that's the way those people are. Feelings over facts."

Jen glanced at her notes.

"Anything else about high school? Or should we move along to college?"

"If I think of other things regarding high school, I'll jot them down for you. Sure, let's talk about college."

"Okay. First of all, why did you choose Dartmouth over all the other colleges and universities you could have attended?"

Pat laughed.

"Because it got me away from home, but not too far away from home. I could drive back to ride Chester when I wanted, for one thing.

"More seriously, though, I was the first in our family to go to college. My dad could have gone, but when I asked him about that, he told me that he had better things to do than to spend years studying subjects he could just as well learn on his own. Nevertheless, he wanted me to go to college if I wanted to and let me choose where.

I looked into lots of colleges and applied to ten, as I recall, but Dartmouth appealed to me the most. Many of the faculty members had great reputations for their critiques of America and for promoting social justice through their teaching and research. That was exactly the environment I wanted."

"That's very important," Jen responded. "Could you tell me about some of the faculty at Dartmouth who had the most influence on you?"

"Good question. I would have to say that the faculty member who affected my thinking the most was history professor Emily Diamond-Ochoa. I took her course on twentieth-century U.S. History. She really drove home to the students how our history was a long parade of oppression of Native Americans, workers, women, minorities—everyone except the white capitalists who controlled the government for their own interests. That was the same message I had heard earlier in high school, but Professor Diamond-Ochoa made it so much more vivid. She also brought in some great outside speakers who were so passionate in their attacks on the mythology of America's greatness.

"Like Ms. Armour, she explained to us that it was imperative to take a side: Either you were for the needed transformation of America, or you were an ally of the capitalist ruling elite. There was no use in arguing against them because they were good at twisting language to deceive and manipulate. All you needed to know about the defenders of capitalism was that they always put profits in front of people. Their rationalizations were built on lies.

"I recall strongly one day in class. Professor Diamond-Ochoa had been talking at length about a book she had just published. It showed how some white guy who had won a Nobel Prize was actually a racist who wanted to keep schools segregated.

"Toward the end of the hour, a student named Vargas—I think he was from Peru—put his hand up and, when called on, said something about a review that argued that she had completely misrepresented the man's views, and quoted others who said that their statements had been edited so as to change their meaning. Then he asked if it wasn't wrong for historians to publish books without making an effort to verify their accuracy.

"Professor Diamond-Ochoa insisted that everything in her book was true, according to *her interpretation*. And she said that the person who wrote that review must be on the payroll of some right-wing think tank and therefore biased against her.

"Then she totally skewered Vargas by asking, 'Why would you insist on being fair toward a segregationist?' To that, he impudently replied, 'But isn't the real question *whether* the man was a segregationist or not?'

"Well, Diamond-Ochoa then said what *needed to be said.* 'Mr. Vargas, you have frequently interrupted this class with your thoughts about property rights and contracts and so on and now you're harassing me over my award-winning book. I think it would be best if you dropped the course NOW.' Vargas looked stunned, then picked up his backpack and walked out. Diamond-Ochoa glared at him until he was out the door, then said to the class, 'Okay, now we can get back to learning about history.' *She really knew how to handle conflict.* It was awesome."

"After the class, I asked Professor Diamond-Ochoa about her book. She said that Vargas was correct in that it had been severely attacked by some right-wing hacks, but that she paid no attention to them. She, after all, was on the right side of history.

In any case, she explained, doing good history was about conveying the right *attitudes* about people and events, not fussing over little details or trying to be fair to people who were allied with the oppressors. Her words have always stayed with me. If you are committed to change, you have to go all in."

Pat took a long drink of her iced tea.

"And the story doesn't end there. Years later, when I was attorney general of California, I found out that that student, Eduardo Vargas, was running a think tank in California. Naturally, it was one of those places that was always putting out criticism of the state's policies, and I thought, 'Wouldn't it be nice to take him down.'

"So my office identified a bevy of regulations his think tank had arguably violated and we filed suit against it. However, Vargas had a sharp lawyer named Bob Barsamian who handled the case and convinced the judge that Vargas' outfit hadn't violated any of the regulations and should recover his attorney fees plus damages. So that case failed and the state had to fork over half a million dollars to the bastard. I hated losing that one."

"That must have stung."

"Yes, it did, but I finally got them both," Pat said gleefully.

"The Justice Department bled Vargas dry with a Hate Speech violation during my first term in the White House. Vargas had to close down his silly little Property Rights and Economic Liberty Center. Maybe he went back to Peru to raise llamas," she said with a laugh.

"As for Barsamian, when I was governor, I was able to get him disbarred for a violation of the law."

"What did he do?"

"He was walking his dog without wearing a face mask during Covid. Someone reported him, and the next day we pounced on him. He was in violation of a government order, and we couldn't have members of the bar association committing such offenses, now could we?"

Pat sat back in her chair and smiled broadly.

"The president of the bar association said that Barsamian hardly deserved to lose his license to practice law over that. But we made it clear to him that if he fought for Barsamian, we'd be investigating *him* next. Naturally, he decided to go along."

"Nothing like the sweet taste of revenge, is there?"

"No, Jen, *there sure isn't*," Pat said, leaning back further in her chair.

Jen took another drink of her iced tea, then said, "Please tell me more about your life at Dartmouth."

"Glad to. Right off the bat, I got involved in College Democrats, the Dartmouth Progressive Alliance, and the Committee to Defend Against Racism. I also signed up for the debate team but only stayed on for one semester. I had taken an English course with a professor, Cecile Eagleton, who argued that it was a myth that there are two sides to every question. That wasn't true, she said. People could *know* what was right from their instincts and sense of fairness. The notion that people should use logic to decide right from wrong was just a tool to privilege the power structure. That resonated with me.

"Professor Eagleton taught us to analyze literature as reflecting nothing more than power struggles, and I realized that debate was rooted in a false conception. Having students argue 'pro' and 'con' merely distorted their consciousness. Professor Eagleton loved my paper, 'Why John Stuart Mill was Wrong.'

"Once I had grasped that 'free speech' was just a cover for unjust power structures, I became active in efforts on campus to prevent people who had harmful ideas from speaking. The Progressive Alliance put up opposition against every speaker who we thought would poison the Dartmouth environment with hate speech. For example, a right-wing group had invited an economics professor to campus to give a talk on racial discrimination in pro sports. Once we found out that he was an advisor to the College Republicans at his school, we knew that we *had* to oppose him.

"We demanded that the administration cancel his appearance, but we got some excuse about Dartmouth's commitment to academic freedom. So we took matters into our own hands. We put up posters encouraging students to stay away because the man was a racist.

"On the night of his speech, about twenty of us were in the front row, waiting for the guy to show up so we could let him know what we thought of him. For more than fifteen minutes, we shouted, interrupted, and waved signs.

"Finally, an administrative official showed up to say that we would either have to listen respectfully or leave the building. Well, we had made our point and decided to leave.

"From that day onward, fighting the power structure and advancing social justice became my principal occupations at Dartmouth."

"Good thing you made that decision. Where would the country be if you hadn't become an activist?"

Pat soaked in the praise and smiled.

"What other courses at Dartmouth had an influence on you?"

Pat gazed out at the Pacific for a moment.

"One very important course was African-American Studies with Professor Armand Green. He taught us that American capitalism was heavily dependent upon slave labor and that since the benefits of slavery were still spread throughout the economy, it was only right to put the cost of reparations on the country as a whole. I agreed with him and implemented reparations when I was in office, as you know.

"Professor Green also ran into trouble-making students on occasion. One day in class, a white student asked him if he would care to respond to a recent newspaper column by a Black professor who was against reparations. Green shot him down in flames, saying that white people had no standing to appropriate the writings of Black people. In any case, that Black professor was a notorious apologist for the white power structure from his tenured chair. His views weren't *authentic* and therefore not worth discussing. I really enjoyed watching that white kid wither in his seat."

"Oh, I can just imagine it. Any other key courses that stand out in your memory?"

"Sure. There was Environmental Justice, Chinese History—Americans have so many misconceptions about Mao—"Misanthropy in Shakespeare," a course on Ableism, and Women's Studies taught by a professor who'd written a bestselling book attacking the glass ceiling. And in my pre-law major, I had some great courses, especially the one on the Living Constitution."

"Any bad courses?"

"Just one that I'd call a total waste. It was a seminar on political theory and the elderly individual who taught it was completely unfair to me on a paper I wrote, so I dropped the class. His name, I think, was Richberg. He was the only professor I was really disappointed with. His views were retrograde and he had us reading works by white, Eurocentric men. I couldn't see why Dartmouth allowed him to keep teaching."

Pat stood up.

"I think it's about time for some lunch, don't you, Jen? I'll have my chef prepare a light California lunch. Some soup and a salad, maybe?"

Jen switched off her recorder and jotted on her notepad, "Emph how education shaped PF's beliefs."

"I have to say that I'm famished. A break for some good food is just what I need."

The former president and the writer enjoyed their lunch, served on elegant china. Their conversation drifted to flowers, the weather, and pets when Pat's gray cat appeared.

After a stroll around the estate and grounds, Pat and Jen sat back down at the table.

Jen began. "Pat, so far we haven't talked about your late husband. I'd like to learn more about him and your marriage."

Pat thought for a moment before answering.

"Certainly. You no doubt know that my husband, Sherman Harth, was a highly successful trial lawyer who specialized in mass torts. He sued for defective products and failure to adequately warn consumers. In fact, this house was built by the founder of a power equipment company that Sherm drove into bankruptcy.

"It was a terrible shock to me when Sherm died three years ago."

"You must miss him very much," said Jen. "His funeral was so moving."

Pat rubbed her hands together.

"I'll be honest with you, Jen. Ours was more a marriage of convenience than of love. Sherm and I got married when I was in the House, and he was an up-and-coming attorney. He had already scored some big hits with multi-million-dollar verdicts for his clients. We happened to meet at a party in Malibu. I was sure that he was going to be a superstar lawyer who'd haul in loads of money, and as you well know, money is the lifeblood of politics. I was certain that we'd make a great team.

"And Sherm recognized me as a rising star in the Democratic Party and figured that my name and influence could help boost his career. During our marriage, we would often go for weeks or even months without seeing each other. I was busy in Washington and his cases took him all over the country. We never had time for children. Sherm's money helped with my campaigns and bought this house, a yacht, and much more. But yes, I do miss him."

Jen nodded to Pat.

"As I recall, he died while windsurfing."

"That's correct. What actually killed him was a burst aneurism. He'd have died whether on land or the sea. Ironically, he had just filed suit against the company that made the equipment he was using on the grounds that its consumer warning was inadequate."

Jen was looking at her notes, about to ask her next question, when Pat spoke again.

"There's something I should have said when we first met, Jen. I meant to say how deeply grateful I am for all the support I received during my career from the media in general and especially your paper.

"The Fourth Estate always helped by shaping public opinion in our favor. Over the years, your own writing—I almost always made time to read your columns—did as much as anyone's to make the conservatives look foolish or venal or both. I'd like to know how you got into journalism."

Jen had a well-rehearsed answer for that.

"Well, when I was young, I really loved music. I played the piano rather well and decided to go to Oberlin, which was famous for its music department. I knew I wasn't good enough to be a soloist but thought I might like to teach music. Funny thing—even though I did study music, what I learned at Oberlin convinced me that I wanted to be a journalist, a journalist who wrote stories that would help change the world.

"Oberlin woke me up the same way those high school and Dartmouth classes did for you. They set my life's course. At first, I freelanced and was lucky that an editor at *The Nation* read one of my pieces and liked it enough to offer me a job. After several years there, I landed a spot at the *Post* and have been there ever since."

"Oh, yes—Oberlin. You must have felt terrible over the way that court case turned out. Those racist Gibsons getting, what was it? Thirty-three million dollars from the jury? What a shame to damage a great college like that.

"If that case had happened in California, I'd have moved mountains to derail the litigation. But Ohio had that moron Republican governor and I suppose he was happy over the whole thing."

As a student, Jen had often patronized Gibson's Bakery when she was a student and never once thought the family had any racist beliefs. But she decided not to mention that and simply said, "Yes, that verdict hurt the school. It could have done so much good with the money."

Pat scowled and shook her head.

"It was *unconscionable*, Jen."

"But I want to go back to a particular instance where good journalism really saved me. Do you remember that town-hall-style debate in Phoenix during my first campaign?"

"Yes, pretty well."

"Then you'll recall how that woman who looked Native American was recognized by the moderator and when she had the microphone, asked, 'You, Governor Farnsworth, have spoken again and again tonight about all the new laws and policies you have in mind, but I have never, tonight or any other time, heard your say anything about laws that you would repeal because they cost too much or interfere with our freedom too much. Could you provide a list of laws you'd repeal, or even one or two?'"

"Yes, I sure do remember that moment. I was watching the debate and thought, 'Oh, this could hurt big time.'"

"That's just what I thought. Her question threw me. I said something like, 'That's a very good question, and I'm glad you asked it.' But what I was thinking at the moment was, 'How the hell did a Navajo or Apache get the idea that we might be better off with a smaller government?'

"How I answered her question, however, was, 'My staff and I have been working on exactly that issue and my campaign will be releasing a white paper on the economy in government soon.'

"I figured that answer would do, but the woman didn't give up the microphone as she was supposed to, and blurted out, 'How can it be that you already have hundreds of pages on your plans to increase the size and cost of the government but don't yet have *anything* on shrinking it?'

"I knew that the whole election could hinge on that one crazy question. At that moment, I realized that if voters started to think about reducing the size of government, that could be the turning point in the campaign since there are still lots of Americans who think the government should be as small and efficient as possible. Fortunately, the moderator asked my opponent, 'Mr. Cosgrove, do you have a list of laws you would like to see repealed?' and he didn't have anything definite either.

"That defused things for the moment but I still sensed danger in the air. For a Native American to ask about cutting back government was extremely problematic. Her question could have caused me real trouble with voters if your paper hadn't figured out how to spin the story to hurt the Republicans."

Jen laughed.

"Yes, that was the brilliant work of one of my colleagues, Kim Adderley. She pounded out a column for the next morning with the title 'GOP Plants Hostile Questioner to Twist Town Hall Debate.' I remember that she cited 'sources' who had said that a tactic the Republicans were using was to infiltrate campaign events like the one in Phoenix with people who looked to be minority and presumably friendly to Democratic candidate Pat Farnsworth, but who were paid to disrupt events with hostile, impertinent questions.

"Almost instantly, CNN and the other networks picked up that 'Planted Disrupters' line and got people thinking about the 'tradition of GOP dirty tricks' rather than about that woman's actual question about repealing laws.

"A day later, I asked Kim if she really had any evidence that the woman had been planted. 'Of course not,' she responded. Her column, she admitted, was sheer fabrication. In fact, she later managed to get in touch with that woman, a Navajo who lived in Arizona and had no affiliation with any political party, and learned that she really believed that we needed to downsize the government. Still, that was an idea we simply had to squelch."

"Well, it was perfectly done and I have always been grateful."

"Since you've brought up that first election, Pat, it sure was a close battle. I thought you had lost when I fell asleep on my sofa that night. You must have been a nervous wreck. But the next morning, you had pulled ahead in those extremely close states."

Pat laughed.

"Actually, I wasn't worried at all. Local Democratic officials in several key states told my staff that they had boxes of reserve ballots that they'd put in to be counted in the early hours of the morning. They assured us that they would have enough votes, and they did.

"What really paid off for us was the money we had invested in winning secretary of state elections two years previously. If you wondered why we were spending millions on winning those offices, it was because we wanted people we could trust to tilt the playing field our way for my presidential campaign. That was perhaps the savviest political investment of all time. So, when precincts in Philadelphia and Detroit and Milwaukee reported in with results like 'three thousand for

Farnsworth, zero for Cosgrove,' that was just what I knew would happen.

"Then, in the ensuing recounts and litigation, the press again helped to secure my victory by calling every report of so-called vote fraud as debunked 'fake news' spread by desperate Republicans. That damped down the uproar and probably pushed Cosgrove to finally concede defeat."

Jen knew that Pat's first election was clouded in controversy over the results in several states, but had not expected to hear the former president admit that the vote totals had been manipulated to ensure her victory. That didn't bother her. The whole idea of the Electoral College was unfair, and if it took manufactured votes to overcome it and give the people the president that a majority wanted, that was just the way things had to be. It was good that Farnsworth hadn't let the rules of the political game get in the way of the one thing that truly mattered, the transformation of America.

Farnsworth interrupted Jen's train of thought, asking. "Shall we go on with the interview, Jen?"

The two then discussed Farnsworth's years at Stanford Law School, which she had chosen because she thought that California was the ideal state for a progressive activist. She hadn't been on the law review, Farnsworth explained, due to the heavy time commitments she had to a host of progressive causes. And, as at Dartmouth, many professors helped stoke her activism.

They proceeded to discuss her career after law school, which began with five years working for a non-profit environmental group that sued to block almost any proposed construction in the state, and then five years as a staff attorney for the Democratic Party. Those ten years of employment qualified Farnsworth for the provision in the federal student loan law that eliminates student debt after ten years of public service work. That saved her over $100,000.

When the incumbent in a Democratic House district decided to retire, Farnsworth jumped at the chance, and with strong backing from environmental groups and public sector unions, won the nomination. In that district, the Democratic nomination was the same thing as winning the seat, and she began her life as a member of Congress. It was in her third term that she met and married Sherman Harth.

During those years, the House was under Republican control, so the bills Pat introduced always died in committee. She wasn't getting anything done that truly mattered.

Farnsworth introduced her anti-Hate Speech bill every term and it was never even given a hearing. Her Living Wage bill, her bill for mandatory gun buy-backs, her bill to criminalize opposition to union organizing by business owners, and many others suffered the same fate.

She summed up her House experience, saying that she'd come to believe that our democracy had become dysfunctional and needed to be replaced with a system more responsive to the needs of the people. "Our supposedly sacred constitutional checks and balances just get in the way of necessary action," she stated forcefully.

Late in the afternoon, Farnsworth told Jen, "I have an engagement this evening and you're probably very tired, so why don't we stop here. I will have Jurgen drive you to your hotel. I believe we have you booked into the Ritz. We can cover more ground tomorrow when we're both well rested."

Jen was glad to hear that. Her day *had* been very long.

The drive to the Ritz-Carlton at Dana Point took just a few minutes. Jen checked in, and the manager escorted her to the suite that had been reserved for her. It looked out over the Pacific. She had a shower, sprawled on the California-King-sized bed, then ordered dinner from the room service menu.

After eating, she checked her phone for messages—urgent only. There *was* one from her research assistant, Greg Stein, with the information she'd asked for to back up a column she was working on.

"Thanks, Greg," she replied and was about to send the email when she had another thought. "Would you please see if you can track down some people who knew President Farnsworth when she was in college, in law school, working as an attorney, etc."

Jen hit "send" and then went back to her balcony to watch the sunset.

CHAPTER 4

Pat Farnsworth and the Transformation of America

"Good morning!" trilled Pat as Jen entered the great house. "I hope you enjoyed your evening. I'm ready to go. Coffee is on the veranda...a delectable roast that I got addicted to in the White House. I'm sure you'll like it. Of course, it's fair trade."

"That sounds just perfect, Pat. I'm really looking forward to our time together today."

The two women settled in at the same chairs they had occupied on the previous day. Jen placed her purse and sun hat beneath hers. She took a sip of her coffee and then said, "Today, I'd like to cover your presidency, Pat. What do you regard as your most important achievements?"

Pat smiled and put down her coffee cup.

"I would have to say that my most important achievement, the one that made almost everything else possible, was the packing, or as I prefer to say, *revitalization*, of the Supreme Court. Without that, little else could have gone as planned.

"First, however, we had to get control of the Senate. As you'll remember, after I was elected, the Republicans held a fifty-one to forty-nine seat majority. Most of the country thought I would be stymied by that, but as luck would have it, Senator Walters of New Hampshire, a Republican, suffered a fatal heart attack in January. Everyone assumed that Governor Mallinois—Jack Mallinois—would appoint another Republican.

"I called Jack—he was so proud of his French ancestry and spoke fluent French—and offered him the ambassadorship to France if he would appoint an independent to the Senate seat, an 'independent' I could trust to caucus with the Democrats. He took the deal and appointed my suggested person, University of New Hampshire president Martin Davies, to the seat. He announced this was a proper move because New Hampshire was an evenly divided state, and Davies was known for his intellectual integrity.

"Of course, Mallinois soon flew off to Paris and Senator Davies, our 'independent,' decided to vote with us to organize the Senate. Republicans howled bloody murder, but they couldn't do anything about the coup I had engineered.

With control of the Senate in hand, we promptly eliminated the filibuster. The Republicans were, therefore, powerless and the time was ripe for bold action to ensure that the Court would not be an obstacle in any of the elements of my plan to transform the nation."

Pat paused to sip her coffee.

"But Pat, didn't some senior Democrats say that it might not be wise to get rid of the filibuster in case the Republicans should at some point regain power?"

"Oh, yes—a few did, but I told them to forget about that because the Republicans were whipped and we would make sure that they could *never* come back. I'd say that the elections since have proven me right...wouldn't you agree, Jen?"

She nodded vigorously. Pat was right. The Republicans had continued to lose seats in Congress, and in her reelection bid, Pat had carried forty-three of the fifty-two states.

"So, with the historic opportunity facing me, I decided to nominate six new justices for the Court, all of whom I knew would be faithful to our principles. They all believed that the Constitution was a *living document* that must be interpreted in light of the nation's current needs, not as a bunch of rich white men, some of whom owned slaves, saw things in 1787.

"I wanted new justices committed to social justice, not antiquated legal notions. Having a large majority on the Court—justices who would approve of the legislation and regulation I had in mind—was crucial.

"Also, those new justices at long last gave us a Court that looked like America, with representatives of all our key demographic groups. Only two of them had been judges before—and three weren't lawyers at all—but nothing requires that members of the Supreme Court have any particular qualifications. The Court was now almost half women and minorities. Most importantly, though, the new justices had the right views on the role of the government. They wanted to expand the rights of people, to ensure equality and safety, and to build a country we could all be proud of.

"Since the revitalization of the Court, right-wing legal groups have stopped bothering with suits to challenge our policies, knowing that they will lose. You know how those outfits used to attack federal power over the environment, for example, claiming that EPA regulations improperly took private property? Well, after a string of eleven to four defeats, those suits have dried up. Same for suits over educational policy, privacy, guns, and other issues.

"One big point I learned in my Con Law class at Stanford was that hotly contested points become 'settled law' after the Court has ruled often enough. Back in the 1930s, conservatives challenged what FDR was doing, arguing that his policies involved unconstitutional spending and delegation of power. After the Court ruled against them in a string of cases, they just gave up. The same thing has happened with regard to the First Amendment. It's now settled law that the government can regulate speech in the public interest. As I said before, the conservatives are beaten and they know it.

"With the Court on our side, we were able to proceed with our reforms without any impediment."

"Pat," Jen interjected, "many have compared your presidency with FDR. Didn't he also want to pack the Supreme Court?"

"Yes, that's correct, but he had a lot of Democrats who were pretty reactionary. Great as he was, he couldn't control them, so his plan went nowhere; things were different for me, though. Senate Majority Leader Dzerzhinsky made it clear that if any members of the Democratic caucus had reservations about packing the Court, they needed to go along for the good of the Party—or else face well-funded primary challenges. They all went along.

"And we had to have a Supreme Court that could issue advisory opinions and overrule old precedents we disliked, without waiting for cases to reach it.

"In the past, you see, the Court never ruled unless it had before it a 'case or controversy' as the Constitution reads, which meant that it couldn't rule until a case made its way through the lower courts, with parties advocating for both sides. Our new Chief Justice, Allison Devereaux—who had succeeded me as Attorney General of California—announced within a week that the Court had adopted new rules to allow it to issue advisory opinions and to review old decisions on its own. How the right-wing squawked about that! But there was nothing they could do to stop the wheels of progress."

"This is fascinating, Pat. Please go on."

Pat sipped her coffee, then continued.

"Well, one of Allison's changes was that the Attorney General of the United States or any state attorney general could request a review of any prior decision of the Court. Requests naturally began pouring in, and the Chief decided which ones to review. Her decisions were based on this calculus: Did the old case obstruct the ability of the government to bring about needed reforms? If so, she would assign a justice to brief the Court on why the decision should stand or be overruled.

"The first such review was of a 1925 case, *Pierce v. Society of Sisters*. It was requested by the attorney general of Oregon. The state wanted to require all students to attend its public schools, just as the state had mandated in its old law that the Supreme Court had declared unconstitutional.

"By ten to five, the Court declared that *Pierce* was overruled. That enabled the state to enact legislation compelling all students to go to public schools. Now all kids in Oregon get the same schooling, schooling that emphasizes their civic responsibilities and teaches them to cooperate rather than compete. Quite a few states have followed Oregon's lead. Since then, the Court has overruled dozens of old decisions that could have been cited as precedent by the opponents of progress, including that Second Amendment case holding that individuals have a right to own guns, the case holding that public workers can't be required to pay union dues, and that terrible *Citizens United* case that allowed unregulated campaign expenditures."

"I can see that the clearing away of old precedents was very important, Pat. Now explain to me about advisory opinions, if you would. I'm not at all familiar with that."

"Of course. In the old days, as I said before, courts only ruled on the constitutionality of statutes after a case based on the law had come before it, with parties arguing for and against. But Chief Justice Devereaux and I thought that wasn't necessary because the Court could decide perfectly well whether a statute was constitutional or not on its own. She declared that the living Constitution shouldn't be hindered by antiquated concepts.

"The first law we wanted to test and get approval for was our Anti-Hate Speech Act. Congress quickly passed it, I signed it, and we sent it to the Court for review. If right-wingers attacked the law as violating the First Amendment, we knew we'd prevail with the new Court—but why put the country through years of needless bickering and litigation over a law we *knew* was good? Why give judges who held 'Originalist' views a shot at delaying the law's implementation?

"We couldn't wait on the slow legal system, while hate speech was infecting America and getting in the way of my National Unity Project. We needed the Court's approval of the law immediately."

Jen nodded to Pat and said, "I remember writing a column praising the Chief Justice for her far-sightedness. She was so correct in saying that while freedom of speech was important, it was equally important to make sure that it was exercised responsibly, not in ways that belittled people, made them feel unwanted or unsafe, or which spread falsehoods. Former President Obama had made that argument in his book *A Promised Land*. Democracy can't really function when citizens are deluged with erroneous information and extreme opinions."

"I *loved* that column, Jen," Pat replied, clasping her hands together.

"As you know, our National Commission to Prevent Hate Speech was and remains a key component of the National Unity Project. We are concerned about the general welfare of *all Americans* and therefore can't allow hateful speech by a few to get in the way. Under Chairman Mortain, the Commission has done a lot to clean up our national discourse. False and demeaning speech is being treated as the national menace it is."

Jen cleared her throat.

"Some conservatives argue that the National Commission targets their speech whether it contains anything the slightest bit hateful or not, while ignoring completely hateful speech by people on our side. How do you respond to that criticism?"

"Let them complain all they want to," Pat retorted.

"If they don't like having to defend themselves in front of the Commission, they can either find non-hateful ways of speaking or just shut up. In fact, it seems that many have done just that, from the closure of a large number of their magazines and websites.

"And besides, public opinion polls show strong support for the Commission. We began it with a campaign to sell the people on the need to stop hate speech, and the stream of media stories on the bad speech that we have fined has only increased that support.

"As one of my Dartmouth professors put it, 'The worst abuse of power is to fail to use it for good.' That's what we're doing—using power for good."

"That's so true, Pat. I'll use that line. Could we move on and talk about another big part of your National Unity Project, namely the Commission on Statues, Names, and Art?"

"With pleasure, Jen."

"From my initial listening tour of America, one thing I learned was how terribly important it was to many people—and not just people of color—to cleanse the country of divisive, hurtful reminders of our past so that we could get on with the building of a truly just nation. In order to do that, we *had* to tear down offensive statues, rename buildings that celebrated evil people, eliminate public art that was demeaning, and so on. That work had begun before my administration, but it wasn't a coordinated, national effort. I knew that it had to be, so just two months into my first term, I issued an executive order creating the Commission.

"It swung into action, compiling lists of things to be considered for removal, renaming, or destruction. I appointed a woman I admired, Constance Bailey, a professor of American Studies at the University of Michigan, to head up the Commission. It took evidence from activists around the country who had been impacted by offensive things. If it was convinced that action was warranted, the Commission issued appropriate orders.

"If it was a statue, a demolition firm was contracted; if it was a building, the owner was notified that the offensive name would have to be removed; if it was public art, the Commission ordered it painted over, taken away, or whatever other remedy was best. Immediately, the country became a beehive of activity to rid ourselves of offensive things."

Pat tilted her head upward in an air of triumph.

"I wrote a column on the Commission's deliberations. From what I could tell, most of the items that the Commission considered were scheduled for destruction or renaming, but not all. Do you know why that was, Pat?"

Pat laughed.

"That's easy. Connie Bailey and I thought it would look best if around ninety percent of the items that were evaluated were destroyed or otherwise acted upon, but around ten percent allowed to remain. That was to create the appearance of fairness and objectivity, which we thought would help build public support. We made sure to get all the really big, white supremacist and militaristic things, but left some obscure and fairly inoffensive things. We allowed a statue of Ethan Allen to stay, for example, even though a group of Vermont socialists insisted that it should go because his views on private property were problematic."

"I thought that the news reports of statue demolition were very uplifting. You'd see a crowd of diverse Americans standing around and cheering as a statue was toppled and hauled away, or a mural celebrating some aspect of our racist past was painted over, never to demoralize people again. It was wonderful to see. I was finally proud to be an American.

"Jen, you'll probably remember that some of America's perennial gripers said that the Commission's work was a huge waste of money, but we responded that it was absolutely crucial for the nation's healing to get rid of hurtful and divisive symbols. Besides, all the workers were getting paid well as required by law, so it was actually a stimulus for the economy."

Pat paused, and Jen had a question at the ready.

"Mount Rushmore was a special problem, wasn't it?"

"Yes, it sure was. A large number of people in that area of South Dakota didn't want to see the faces of the four presidents demolished, saying that the monument drew the tourists who provided their livelihood. Fans of the monument sent in loads of letters and petitions to the Commission not to place it on the To Be Destroyed list.

"But as I explained in my second State of the Union address, Mount Rushmore was an affront to modern America as it celebrated white male domination as well as the mistreatment of Native Americans. Some people suggested adding Barack Obama and Oprah Winfrey, but even if that had been feasible, it wouldn't have solved the problem of honoring two slaveholders.

"Removing the faces and repairing the mountain—now called Six Grandfathers Mountain as the Sioux did before white men intruded—took two years. It is still a national park but I hear that very few people go there now. It's too bad about the people who lost their livelihoods, but we had to think of the greater good."

Pat poured herself another cup of coffee. Jen watched her warily then took a deep breath and asked, "What about the Star Spangled Banner? Can we talk about that?"

"Definitely. It had to go too. The Star-Spangled Banner glorified war and all that stuff about freedom and bravery—so utterly out of date and out of alignment with the values of the new America. We did some polling that showed a substantial percentage of Americans felt 'triggered' by the song and that was unacceptable. Our new anthem—celebrating diversity, security, and togetherness—is much, much better.

"Of course, there was some opposition," Pat continued.

"The owners of a few pro sports teams wanted to continue playing the Star-Spangled Banner before games, but my secretary of the treasury, Simon Sudbury, informed them that any team that played the old anthem at any time would lose eligibility for federal stadium subsidies. They saw the light then!

"Now games begin with the new anthem, 'Our Beautiful Home.' I've been told that very few fans participate in singing it and many turn around and bend over as their sign of defiance. It's so petty and childish, but I think that the opposition will burn itself out in a few more years."

Pat reached for her coffee cup, and Jen asked, "How about the flag? There was also talk about changing it, but nothing has happened."

Pat sighed.

"My advisors and I discussed that endlessly. Some said that the flag was a bad symbol of the America we wanted to leave behind; others said that even though it was regarded by many as a symbol of hate, trying to change it would be too costly politically.

"The latter side convinced me that we were doing enough to change the country and didn't need to whack this huge hornet's nest. Perhaps one of my successors in office will be able to change the flag. We've been preparing the way. For example, a pair of researchers at the University of Illinois recently published a study showing that seeing images of the Stars and Stripes is associated with implicit bias against minorities. I'd say that was federal grant money well spent, wouldn't you, Jen?"

"I certainly would, Pat. And now could we talk about our two new states? In the past, there was *discussion* among Democrats of making the District of Columbia and Puerto Rico states, but you were the one who got it done."

"Thanks for your good words, Jen. You're correct that previous Democratic administrations had toyed with the idea, but they didn't have the political power that I did. With a united Congress and no filibuster, it was easy. Why shouldn't we add four reliable Democratic senators and make the electoral college easier for us?"

"Absolutely," said Jen as she refilled her coffee cup.

She knew, however, that statehood had meant another layer of taxes on her city to support a governor, lieutenant governor, and more bureaucracy. The old license plates complaining about 'Taxation Without Representation" had been replaced with colorful new ones, but quite a few people were quietly saying that statehood had made things worse for residents of the old District of Columbia.

Not only did it cost more to live in Federal City, as Washington, D.C. was now officially called, but the place had grown increasingly unsafe. The street panhandlers were getting more aggressive, and robberies were more numerous. Residents like herself were spending more money to install bulletproof windows and reinforced doors.

Just a month ago, there had been a mass shooting in an African-American area of the city, leaving six dead and fifteen wounded. That event had only received local coverage, and Jen knew why—the media didn't bother with shootings unless they were useful to the Democrats, which this one wasn't.

But the problems of living in the nation's capital weren't relevant to the biography, so Jen decided to go on to her next question.

"Pat, safety was one of the main themes of your administration and protection from gun violence was the centerpiece. Your gun buyback program was instrumental in taking thousands of guns off the streets. Tell me more about that."

"Happy to do so, Jen. Ever since my days in the House, I had wanted to attack the problem of guns, but the Second Amendment freaks kept blocking my efforts. They just don't care about the lives lost every year, and their fixation on the

Second Amendment is so foolish. They kept yammering about an 'individual right' to own firearms, but once the Supreme Court had overruled its case holding that there was such a constitutional right, the way was cleared for my new law. We were, at last, able to put the common good above those individual rights claims.

"There were already laws meant to keep potentially dangerous people from obtaining a gun, but never had we made a concerted effort to *reduce* the number of guns in society. The law I signed mandated that Americans turn in all guns they owned to agents at federal gun collection centers, with the exception of ornamental antiques, as carefully defined in the statute. But we didn't want to be accused of taking private property without compensation, so we set a price of $100 per gun. Experts said that would be reasonable.

"My political model for this was FDR's gold seizure of 1933. He understood that the country had to get past the days of using gold as money, and I understood that we had to get past the days of using guns to settle disagreements.

The results of the law were dramatic. Federal agents in the Bureau of Alcohol, Tobacco, Firearms and Explosives collected thousands and thousands of guns. Mountains of them!

"They were trucked to regional centers for destruction. I was on hand for the first gun destruction party, as I liked to call them, in Los Angeles. I really appreciated the way you and other writers covered the results of the program with headlines like, 'Finally, Serious Action on Guns.'

"It's true that shootings sometimes still occur, but that's why the second phase of the mandatory buyback is needed, with its emphasis on *mandatory*. Federal agents are beginning to search for and confiscate weapons that weren't turned in during the buyback phase. Those who thought they could just keep their guns hidden are finding out that there are serious penalties for violating the law."

"Haven't some civil liberties types complained about the searches? What's your response to them, Pat?"

"I say that the Fourth Amendment is good, that we need to keep government officials from conducting improper, warrantless searches. But gun violence is a *national emergency*. The Supreme Court issued an advisory opinion to allow our agents to search under general warrants, meaning that if the Attorney General finds that is was an undue amount of gun violence in a county, agents could search anywhere in that county. We think it strikes the right balance between Fourth Amendment values and the need to make the country safe.

"We're bringing in more guns, and also arresting many people who thought they could ignore the law. Each year of my presidency, we expanded the budget for our anti-gun efforts, and I trust that President Barlow will continue doing so until the gun problem is finally solved."

"What about people who make new guns or smuggle them in from abroad? How did you deal with that?" asked Jen.

"For anyone who does that, the law's most severe penalties apply—solitary confinement for life. And we have added new prison space for exactly that," Pat added in a triumphant tone.

At that moment, one of the former president's aides approached the table and said to her, "Madam President, you have a call regarding your Presidential Library. Would you care to take it?"

Pat nodded to him and then turned to Jen. "This call is pretty important. Please excuse me for a few minutes."

Jen nodded back. She could use the time to check her messages.

One was from Greg Stein. He had located a few people who had known Pat Farnsworth earlier in her life. Jen glanced at the first two on his list. One was Nicole Swensen, who had been her roommate at Dartmouth and the second was Alexander Oistrakh, who had been one of her law school professors. Greg had included email addresses and phone numbers for them. Jen thought that the book would be more interesting if it included insights from people who weren't part of the political world. Talking to people like these two would be useful.

Jen wrote back to Greg, "Good work. I'll be back in town next week."

Next, Jen checked the local weather. The forecast called for partial clouds and brisk winds in the afternoon and into the evening. That was good, since Jen had decided on going to Laguna Beach after finishing up with Pat.

A trolley ran from the Ritz-Carlton up to the town, a few miles north along the Pacific Coast Highway. Jen's idea was to take the trolley to Laguna Beach, enjoy a nice seafood dinner, then watch the sunset from the beautiful vantage point of Heisler Park, as the cap to a delightful day.

Jen went back to her email and saw one from Maddy. She and her husband Josh were going to order tickets for a concert by the Sturtevant String Quartet on Saturday evening, she'd written. Should they also get one for her?

Maddy and Josh were immersed in music. Maddy, her younger sister of five years, was a much better pianist than Jen had ever been. She taught piano in and around Alexandria, Virginia. Josh was a good cellist who had inherited his family's long-established music store in Alexandria. White's Music sold instruments, sheet music, and musical knick-knacks such as busts of composers. Jen was happy that her little sister had made such a good life for herself.

The concert sounded very appealing, with quartets by Haydn, Schubert, and Franck. Much as she'd enjoy the concert ordinarily, Jen figured that she would be too tired and wrapped up in the biography to truly enjoy the music. She replied to Maddy, "Wish I could but don't think I can make it. Really sorry. You know how much I like Franck's great quartet."

While Pat was gone, Jen read things on her favorite websites. Often, she got ideas for her columns that way.

Finally, Pat walked back onto the veranda.

"Sorry that took so long, Jen. It's time for a bite of lunch, don't you think?"

"I couldn't agree more, Pat."

Pat motioned to someone waiting at the door, then said, "How about a stroll around the grounds while lunch is being prepared?" Jen nodded and put on her wide-brimmed hat, a necessity in the bright California sun.

"That's a good idea, Jen – I ought to start wearing a hat myself, now that I can get out in the sun more."

During their walk, Pat dominated the conversation, telling Jen about her plans for improving the landscaping around the house, adding a rose garden in one place and a koi pond in another. Jen thought to herself that with California in a drought, it was a touch unseemly for the former president to be so lavish with the use of water. Naturally, she kept those thoughts to herself.

After a delectable lunch, the two resumed their interview.

Jen began by asking, "One of your main themes was to create an economy that's equitable for everyone, Pat. Let's discuss the major components of your efforts to make that a reality."

"Yes indeed, let's talk about that," Pat replied with enthusiasm.

"I think that the place to begin is my Universal Basic Income program. Far too many deserving Americans were falling through the cracks of the old welfare system, so we came up with UBI. Now everyone below the Decent Living Threshold automatically receives money from the Federal Reserve—what some are calling 'fedcoin.'

"The people love it. We had congressional hearings where everyday Americans testified about their struggles to get by, especially with prices rising so quickly. UBI patches up our frayed social safety net.

"Another key thing was our tax reform. We not only made the income tax more progressive—the rich are now *closer* to paying their fair share—but we instituted a wealth tax for the first time. I cringe at the thought of billionaires enjoying so much while most Americans have to scrimp to get by—and so do most voters. No one needs that much money, and we're now taxing it to be used for the good of all.

"And a third component was our minimum wage plus law. As you probably know, Jen, going back to the 1930s, the federal government set the minimum wage for newly hired workers. Paying a worker less was a violation of the law.

"But economists on my team identified a weakness, namely that there was no law to assist workers *beyond that initial wage.* While some got raises, others remained stuck at the minimum. It's both depressing and economically damaging to see fellow workers moving up while you're stuck at the minimum wage.

"So we changed the law to require employers to give workers raises on a fixed schedule. No workers are left behind. They start at a minimum of twenty dollars and must receive semiannual raises of at least a dollar an hour. That's really boosting their earnings and, at the same time, it's a benefit for companies because their workers have more to spend on their products. What worked for Henry Ford is now working for all businesses across America.

A fourth thing we did was to take California's far-sighted law called AB 5 and make it national policy. The so-called 'gig economy' of short-term work like driving for Uber, was not right for most of the people in it. They didn't have the employer-provided benefits—health, dental, vision, psychiatric counseling—that they needed. Companies were able to get away with hiring workers on the cheap by calling them 'independent contractors.' We tightened the law so that companies can no longer do that. We're making companies act in a socially responsible way."

Jen knew people who used to drive for Uber but lost their jobs after the national law went into effect and now had no earnings at all, just their UBI benefits. But as Pat said, the government must act for the overall good. That's what good leaders did—they used the power of the government to achieve important national objectives.

Jen wanted to move on to another of Pat's big achievements and asked, "Would you say, Pat, that your free college program was also a part of your economic plan?"

"Oh, very much so, Jen. A college education today is really essential if a young American wants to have a successful life. More and more jobs require a college degree, and statistics show that, on average, people who have college degrees earn more than a million dollars more during their working careers than do people without them.

"Unfortunately, some people couldn't afford college. To make things equitable for them, as well as to inject more talent into the economy, I pushed through my free college program. Just as with our single-payer national health plan, we now have single-payer college.

"Enrollments have increased, and the U.S. is on the verge of gaining the top spot in terms of the percentage of its people who have college degrees. Nothing could be more important for our prosperity and national competitiveness.

"But there are other aspects of my free college program that aren't about money, Jen. On average, college grads are healthier and are more civic minded. And they're certainly *better people* for having studied diversity and gone through anti-bias training, as is now mandated by federal regulations. More Americans are going to college, and colleges are giving them a more comprehensive education than in the past."

"That is a key point, Pat," Jen interjected.

"I know how much Oberlin transformed my life. It's good for America that more young Americans are getting the same experience that we did, with dedicated, passionate professors. Madame President, you made it happen and the country will continue to reap the benefits as more and more of our people absorb the right views."

As Pat leaned back and soaked up the praise, Jen continued:

"You just mentioned federal regulations a minute ago, Pat. You used the power of the Department of Education far more than any of your predecessors, didn't you? Let's spend some time on that."

"Yes, I did. Previous Democratic administrations had made some rather timid use of the Department, such as Obama's changes in Title IX enforcement, but they lacked, well, *guts*. They were held back by the courts, but we took care of that problem. With my full support, Secretary of Education Alexis Danvers went in with a mission to improve education from pre-K through grad school. Through her guidance letters, she was quickly able to accomplish a lot—weeding out unqualified teachers, making student discipline more equitable, strengthening the curriculum by mandating the inclusion of materials from the '1619 Project,' and removing books that contained offensive language or stereotypes. She also mandated that all faculty and staff must participate in training to counter implicit bias and microaggressions.

"At the same time, many of the states were doing more to regulate their education systems by cracking down on private schools that were not in compliance with health and safety rules, and arresting homeschooling parents who had avoided proper certification. As a result, we now have a much higher percentage of students in safe, professionally staffed public schools than at any time in our history. All of that bodes very well for our future, doesn't it?"

"No doubt about it, Pat."

"If we could shift to a different subject now, I would like to talk about your efforts at controlling inflation. It accelerated throughout your terms in office and prices are now increasing by fifty percent each year. Some people in your own party have been saying that you weren't as aggressive as you should have been in fighting inflation. What do you say?"

Pat leaned forward in her chair. Her expression turned sour. She thought for a moment before answering.

"As you know, Jen, many nations throughout history have suffered from bouts of inflation. They seem to come and go like outbreaks of disease, and try as government officials might, they can't always be contained.

"What I learned in college economics and the best economists in the world, including many Nobel Prize winners, is that inflation occurs when businesses feel the antisocial need to increase their profits. The rising inflation we have experienced for the last eight years is, I am certain, a reaction by greedy businessmen to my efforts at building a fair and just nation. The media, especially your paper, has put out story after story on the business owners responsible for the plague of inflation—those 'economic royalists' as FDR called them. They lack conscience. It isn't easy for the government to deal with a pandemic of greed like that.

"We did take the steps that our leading economists recommended. We established the Price Stabilization Board to set guidelines for appropriate prices and then we made the guidelines mandatory, with fines for violators.

"But corporate greed raged on. I used several of my State of the Union speeches to denounce the avaricious and praise the economic heroes who were obeying the guidelines. Yes, some young firebrands in the party wanted to see criminal sanctions for the people who are responsible for price increases, and a few of them advocated that we do away with the capitalist price system entirely—but I didn't think America was quite ready for that. The *concept* is good, but I thought more groundwork had to be laid first.

"For now, we must coexist with capitalism, but always be vigilant against the greed of the capitalists. But I can tell you that President Barlow has a team working on a plan called The Great Reset that will finally put an end to laissez-faire and bring in a scientifically planned economy. I think we will see that during her first term."

Pat looked out over the Pacific Ocean. Jen sensed that she was about to shift mental gears.

"It's a sad fact of life, Jen, that political leaders are often blamed for things beyond their control, like inflation. That had always been in the back of my mind earlier in my career, but being president really drove it home. I did everything I could to fix America's problems, but people were attacking me for not fixing the innate greed of business owners and landlords and the rest of that class. I could and did take the heat. It's part of the job of being president—using power in ways that make some people unhappy so the nation can advance."

For the rest of the afternoon, Jen and Pat discussed other issues that had been important during her presidency: her fair housing policy that broke down suburban segregation, her environmental policies that ended the scourges of gasoline-powered cars, fracking, and disposable packaging, her policies to reinvigorate the union movement by cracking down on businesses that opposed collective bargaining, her Federal Office of Innovation (which was created to prevent businesses from using new methods and technologies without first obtaining the government's approval),her federal TV initiative, which brought free news and entertainment programming to anyone who signed up, her Reparations for Slavery payments, her executive order mandating training for all federal workers in avoiding pronoun misuse, her excess profits tax on businesses, her Feed America program that had put federal food stores in areas that had been deemed 'food deserts' and which, Pat happily reported, were rapidly expanding into other areas as for-profit grocery chains went bankrupt, her bailouts of state governments that ran out of money, and her aggressive foreign trade policies that had kept cheap, unfairly priced products out of the U.S.

In all, Pat chortled, she had done more than any previous president to use the federal government to bring order and progress to the people. Jen jotted that down in her notepad.

After they had finished, Pat walked with Jen back through her home to the waiting SUV. The winds had picked up and Jen had to reach up to her head to keep her hat on.

"Do have a wonderful evening, Jen," said Pat. "We will continue talking tomorrow at ten, if that suits you."

"That will be just perfect, Pat. Thank you for another great day."

CHAPTER 5

Will Collier

Jurgen pulled the presidential SUV to a stop in front of the Ritz. Jen got out and walked inside, carrying her hat and purse.

She went straight to the concierge desk and asked if he could recommend a seafood restaurant in Laguna Beach. He gave her the name of the one he thought she'd like best and asked if he could make a reservation for her. She said yes, for six o'clock. Then she asked him about the trolley into town and the concierge replied that the nearest stop was just a short walk down the hill from the entrance to the hotel. He also told her which trolley stop in town was closest to the restaurant.

Jen went to her room to change clothes, choosing white slacks, an orange blouse, and her bright blue windbreaker. She then walked back through the hotel and outside, down the hill, to the trolley stop. In about five minutes, the trolley arrived.

On the ride, Jen thought about the progress she was making on getting the material for the book. Another couple of days with Pat would do it; after that, she would dig into presidential papers and contact the people on Greg's list. Writing this book was going to be *enjoyable*. Pat Farnsworth was great to talk to, and what a fighter she was.

Jen got off the trolley at the stop the concierge had suggested and walked a block to the restaurant, arriving just before six.

The *maitre'd* greeted Jen and asked if she would like a window table that looked out over the ocean. She readily agreed, and he seated her at a table with a spectacular view out toward the Pacific. Looking around the restaurant, she saw only two other tables occupied. She thought it strange that the best seafood restaurant in Laguna Beach was nearly empty but dismissed the thought once the waiter brought the menu.

Jen ordered clam chowder, planked salmon, and asparagus. Feeling very content, she also ordered a bottle of their best *sauvignon blanc*. Why not enjoy everything to the fullest?

A whole bottle of wine was a bit much for Jen, but she was in a blissful mood and besides, the paper was covering her expenses.

Every bite of the food was superb. When Jen was finished eating, she went to pay and noticed that the restaurant was still nearly empty.

After her meal, Jen stepped out into the breezy early evening and walked the short distance to Heisler Park, a beautiful park on the cliffs overlooking the ocean. She thought about strolling along the trail along the edge, but instead, decided to take a bench with a view straight out to the ocean for what she was certain would be a spectacular sunset. That was all she felt like doing at the moment.

Years ago, Jen had vacationed in the area, staying with her college friend Tracy McGlocklin who worked for an advertising agency just to the north in Huntington Beach. They had enjoyed the lively towns along the coast, but nothing had compared with the amazing sunset they had taken in at Heisler Park.

Tracy had died in a horrific car crash eight years ago. Jen still hadn't gotten over that. Her thoughts were bittersweet.

The sun was going down and the wind was picking up strongly. A gust blew her hat off her head and it might have sailed right over the cliff if it hadn't gotten caught on the branch of a cypress tree. Jen ran after it and once she had the hat back in her grasp, pushed it firmly down on her head.

Seated back on the bench, Jen took in the slow-moving kaleidoscope that the sky had become with patches that looked like molten copper, streaks of blue, a river of orange, dabs of pink, and blotches of white. The intensity of the colors was like no sunset she had seen since that last day with Tracy.

Jen also recalled great sunsets she had seen as a child. Her parents often took Maddy and her for drives along the Lake Michigan shore to see old lighthouses, buy bags of fresh cherries, and climb the huge sand dunes. At the end of the day, they'd have a picnic of local cheese and bread and fruit, watching the sunset over the lake. Maddy once asked, "Does the lake make the clouds get so colorful?" and her dad explained that it wasn't because of the lake, but the rays of the setting sun bouncing off the clouds.

They had been a happy family. Jen's parents had died too young—first, her mother of cancer and just two years later, her father in a car accident when he had hit a patch of black ice on the highway and spun out of control. Both had always praised her work even though their beliefs and hers were polar opposites. They were stoical, hard-working, loving people, and she missed them.

Too soon, the colors began to fade. Jen sat and savored the sunset until there was nothing more to see, and then she walked back to the trolley stop.

When she got there, however, she saw that the trolley had just left. She considered her options—wait here for the next one in twenty minutes, or walk south through the town and get the trolley at another stop? Walking was by far the better choice since Jen did not like inactivity, and a brisk walk after a day with minimal exercise appealed to her.

As Jen walked along Pacific Coast Highway, she noticed that Laguna Beach had changed markedly since she had last been there. Several stores were closed, with Out of Business signs in their windows and an accumulation of debris in their doorways.

She walked past a restaurant with a single light illuminating a somber scene: Chairs were stacked on tables, and a homeless man had taken over the entranceway with a cardboard box. He stared at her with listless eyes.

In front of what had been a florist's shop, there was a faded sign reading, "For Sale or Lease" with a realtor's number. Next to it was a decrepit photography studio, its windows covered with plywood. At many places, planters that used to be festooned with brilliant flowers were overgrown with weeds.

Laguna Beach had declined shockingly. Jen wondered why.

And then she noticed something else—she was alone. A few blocks back, there had been some people out walking, but now she saw no one ahead on the sidewalk.

Jen decided that she'd had enough exercise. It was time to turn around and head back to the last trolley stop she had passed a few blocks back.

Just as she turned, a gust of wind caught her hat, and it went bouncing along a side street. She ran after it and was about to grab it when she stumbled on some uneven pavement and fell, letting out a small cry as she hit the ground.

Jen was getting up when she was startled to hear a gruff man's voice say, "Well, look at this fancy little lady."

Two men in dark clothing had come up behind her. In the gathering darkness, she couldn't see their faces well, but the knife one was holding was unmistakable, glinting in the dim light of a distant streetlamp.

Jen drew breath to scream, but one of them said, "Keep quiet and we won't have to hurt you." The other man moved around behind her and cupped his large hand over her mouth. Her purse with the mace she always carried was on the ground a few feet away. There was no way to reach it. *She was helpless.*

The man with the knife picked up her purse. Jen stared at him, limp with terror. *What were they going to do?*

She struggled against the man's grip, but his strength was overpowering. He began to drag her back into an alley as the other man walked in front of her, moving the knife back and forth menacingly. In a low, deep voice, he said, "Cooperate with us and you'll be okay, lady." She tried to kick at him, but that was useless.

Jen smelled alcohol on the breath of the man behind her. His horrid body odor, too.

"The door's just behind you, Pete," said the man with the knife. "Let's get her inside and have some fun."

"For sure, Joe," Pete replied with a laugh. "I left the duct tape on the hook, just like last time."

Those words were the most terrifying Jen had ever heard.

Jen was certain that she was about to be raped. She had read that rapists usually didn't kill their victims. *Usually.*

What terrors were ahead inside the building? She struggled to get free, but it was useless.

Jen heard Pete fumbling with the doorknob. Joe, with his knife, was now just inches away from her face.

This can't be happening!

At that moment, a flashlight shone on the three of them. A second later, a gun clicked, and a man said loudly, "You assholes let her go or by God I'll make you sorry."

Jen felt Pete's grip release, and she stumbled to the ground. Her attackers ran away down the alley.

"Are you hurt, ma'am?" asked the man with the gun as he reached out a hand to help Jen up.

"No, I'm okay—thanks to you. Who are you?"

"My name's Willis Collier—everyone calls me Will. I'm not a cop, but I sort of patrol around this area to help my neighbors. Crime has been getting worse and the police are stretched mighty thin. While I was walking, I saw your hat being blown down the street and heard some noise as those punks were molesting you. Here's your hat and your purse."

Taking them, Jen said, "I can't thank you enough...if you hadn't come along, Will...." Her voice trailed off.

"Well, you're safe now. Let's get you back where you belong, Miss...."

"I'm Jennifer Van Arsdale, visiting here from Washington. I'm staying at the Ritz-Carlton at Dana Point. I took the trolley into Laguna Beach for dinner and to watch the sunset."

"It sure was a fabulous sunset. Too bad this had to spoil your evening. C'mon—my car is parked just a little ways away. How about if I give you a ride back to the Ritz, Miss Van Arsdale?"

"I would greatly appreciate that, Will. And please call me Jen."

The two walked back to Pacific Coast Highway and crossed the road. In the light, Jen could see Will clearly. He was a Black man with gray, closely-cut hair. His build was muscular. He wore black trousers and a blue long-sleeved shirt. His gun was tucked behind his back.

"Here's my car," Will said as they approached a make of car that Jen hadn't seen in years.

"Why, this is an Oldsmobile, isn't it, Will? My uncle used to work in the assembly plant in Lansing, Michigan where they were made. But GM stopped making them a long time ago."

"You're right about that. The last Olds was made in 1999 and this baby is one of them. It runs well and I make a point of taking good care of my things."

Will opened the passenger door with a key and motioned for Jen to get in. Then he walked in front of the car. As he did, Jen focused on the gun tucked into his waistband. Will let himself in and then placed the gun under the seat.

Jen had never been so close to one before.

A bit nervously, Jen asked, "Do you know where the Ritz is?"

"Oh, I sure do. I was head electrician there for a long time—retired a couple of years ago. I'll have you there in just a few minutes."

Jen thought for a few seconds. Here she was, riding in a 1999 Oldsmobile with a Black man who had just saved her from a terrible fate. She couldn't just get out at the hotel, say thanks, and walk away forever.

She also wanted to learn about him. What was Will Collier's story?

"Will," she began, "I feel that I owe you my life. I *have to* repay you somehow."

He cut her off. "I won't take any money for doing what any decent human being would have done."

"Okay—no money. But what I'd really like to do is just sit and talk for a while. Please let me buy you coffee and maybe some dessert in the restaurant. *Please, Will.*"

"Now that I'll gladly accept," he replied, glancing over at her.

Will parked his car, and the two of them walked into the lobby. The man at the front desk recognized him and waved, "Hi, Will. Long time no see. How have you been?"

"I've been doing fine, Tom, just fine. How about you?"

The restaurant was mostly empty. The hostess seated Jen and Will at a table next to one of the huge windows that looked out over the ocean. In the moonlight, they could see large waves rolling in.

They ordered coffee, and with only the slightest persuasion from Jen, Will also ordered a slice of blueberry cheesecake. The waitress left, and the two regarded each other for a moment. Will spoke first.

"What brings you out to Laguna Beach, Jen?"

She didn't want to be too specific and replied, "I'm a writer. I'm gathering material for a book on...on the state of the country these days. I was somewhat familiar with this area from a previous visit and thought I'd start here."

"Then I suppose you noticed how bad Laguna Beach has become."

"Pretty shocking," she said, nodding.

"The bitter truth is that most of California has become a basket case, Jen. Americans only see the great golf courses and skyscrapers and pictures of the beaches and they hear about amazing stuff coming out of Silicon Valley and think everything is great here. Actually, the state—I grew up here and have seen it up close and personal—has been decaying for many years. It's like a great old house that looks wonderful, but if you look inside at the foundation, you see that it's rotting away."

The waitress returned with their coffee and Will's cheesecake. She poured coffee for each. Jen thanked her and then returned to Will's question.

"You know, Will, it seemed to me as I was walking in Laguna Beach that the town was looking very run down. I am sure that there weren't any closed businesses or smashed windows when I was here before. What's been going on?"

Will sipped his coffee and thought for a moment.

"The truth is that much of California has been in decline for decades. Only in the last few years has it reached coastal cities like Laguna Beach. We've lost that energy that made the state so famous. We're being suffocated by power-hungry politicians who never seem to think about the long-run effects of what they do.

"They keep piling on ambiguous laws and regulations to the point where almost anything might be illegal, with punishment dished out by small-minded people on a whim.

"It's harder and harder to run a business, to find good workers, to afford a home. People are taxed and regulated to death here. We waste huge amounts on ridiculous stuff like the bullet train and lavish pensions for government workers, but we keep farmers from getting the water they need, and it's almost impossible to build anything due to environmental regulations.

"Our kids get what they call an education in our public schools, but the standards are a joke. Then they go on to college, where they rarely learn anything valuable, and after that they become unemployed because the law requires wages that employers can't afford given their low skills and lousy attitude. But things are great for all the people in the education establishment.

"Electricity has become so expensive that young people find it hard to believe that even the poor used to be able to afford air conditioning all the time. Now it's a luxury that even the middle class has to ration. Same thing with our water restrictions."

Will paused to take a bite of cheesecake. Jen was taken aback by the vehemence of his thoughts about California, but *he lived here*. She waited for him to continue, which he presently did after swallowing his bite.

"You probably didn't even see the ugliest thing in Laguna Beach. Just north of town, there's a tent city for homeless people. The government buys expensive tents for them. Everyone avoids that area if possible, even the police.

"It used to be a residential community—little homes built back in the 1940s. But around twenty years ago, the city was approached by a big tech firm that said it wanted to construct a new campus as they called it on that land. The trouble was that the owners didn't want to sell, so the company went to the city and asked it to acquire the land through something called eminent domain. Do you know anything about that, Jen?"

Jen shook her head and replied, "I've heard of it, but don't know much, Will. Please go on."

"Sure. Eminent domain allows governments to take private property for projects that are supposed to benefit the public, as long as they pay the owners a fair price. The city said that this new tech campus would benefit the public because the company would pay much higher taxes than the homeowners did. So the owners were forced out and compelled to accept what Laguna Beach said was fair compensation. It wasn't, but the area was bulldozed anyway in preparation for the glitzy new construction project."

Jen interrupted.

"So just because the city wanted more in taxes, the owners had their homes taken from them? That hardly seems like something to benefit the public. That's legal?"

Will nodded.

"I'm afraid it is. Back in the nineties, the Supreme Court said that it was all right to use eminent domain to take private property land for projects like this as long as the politicians claimed it would boost the economy and increase tax revenues—which means more money for them to spend. So even if the project wasn't exactly for *public use*, if there was supposed to be some *public benefit*, that satisfied the Constitution."

"Okay, Will, I see your point. But didn't the city officials at least have a good idea? There must have been unmet needs that the government could have addressed with more tax revenue, right?"

"Not really, Jen. If the city politicians had more money, they'd have spent it on gaudy things that *they* like—things that give them photo ops and good publicity, but don't do anything for the average person. What I have learned over my years is that politicians mostly waste money. It would be better left in the hands of the people who earned it."

Jen pondered Will's unexpected hostility to the government. Her political philosophy was premised on the need for government to protect ordinary people against the greedy designs of business, but here was a case where the exact opposite had happened, where business had teamed up with government against ordinary people.

How common was that? And could Will be right that politicians tend to waste money on things that make them look good, things that line the pockets of their supporters? The California "Bullet Train" certainly was a costly fiasco. What if democracy didn't work for the public good, but more for the private good of people with connections? Strange but intriguing ideas.

"I'm glad to know that, Will. It's very disturbing to know that the government can do that to people. And in the end, the whole project obviously turned out to be a flop."

Will gave a snort.

"Yeah, that's putting it mildly. The tech company changed its plans and the plan fell through. The land was vacant until a few years ago when the homeless started taking it over. Now the city gives them tents and port-a-potties. I think it's a revealing story about the effects of politics. Self-supporting owners who cared for their homes get booted out and we wind up with a dangerous homeless encampment that costs the city rather than bringing in more taxes. That's symbolic of what has been happening to the entire state."

Will took a long breath.

"And if you think things look bad here, Jen, you should see inland California. Conditions are like they were in the 1930s—poverty, crime, a feeling of hopelessness. If you want to write a book that will depress people, California is the state to look at."

Will took another bite of his cheesecake, and Jen asked, "Why do you say students get an education in name only, Will? Aren't the schools here held to high standards?"

He swallowed his bite, then replied, "When I was a kid, the schools were fairly good, but about forty years ago, bad ideas started to take hold. One was that students had to have 'self-esteem' in order to learn, so teachers stopped being critical. They stopped giving bad grades when they were deserved. Keeping students happy became more important than making sure they were learning, so learning slowed to a crawl.

"I saw that with my own kids. My wife and I used to go over reports and essays the kids had gotten back—always with an A and a smiley face. But when we read them, we saw lots of errors that the teachers let go—or maybe they didn't even realize were errors. Things like getting the words 'their,' 'there,' and 'they're' mixed up.

"We began correcting their tests and papers ourselves to make sure the kids weren't hopped up on self-esteem they didn't deserve.

"Another part of the problem was discipline. School authorities started to go easy on the disruptive kids, and that just encouraged them to act out even more. Some principals tried to keep order by punishing or even expelling the bad ones, but just about all of them were either Black or Hispanic. That landed *the principals* in trouble because their discipline was 'inequitable.'

"Some geniuses in Washington said that it was discriminatory if some groups were punished more than others. Orders went out requiring 'equal treatment' for Blacks, Hispanics, whites, Asians, and any other groups a school might have. That was just idiotic. *Groups* of people don't act up—*individuals* do, and those individuals who do so need to be properly dealt with. Of course, discipline problems got much worse under that policy since the troublemakers knew that they faced little chance of punishment.

"Maybe discipline was more equal, but students who wanted to learn, no matter what their race, were prevented from doing so by the disruptive kids. Black and Hispanic school officials knew the results of that policy would be bad. It was a case of giving people who had no knowledge and wouldn't suffer any harm from making a stupid decision the power to dictate. That's always a recipe for disaster."

Jen had written about the government's policy on equalizing group punishments, which had seemed like a good idea from her position inside the Beltway, but she couldn't see any reason to doubt Will's argument against it. And his point about people making decisions when they won't suffer adverse consequences if they choose badly made sense. She decided not to interrupt his train of thought.

"What's more, Jen, a lot of what the schools now teach is grievance stuff. My younger daughter is a teacher up in Walnut Creek, and she tells me about the material they have to include now on how terrible America's history was. She knows she'd get in trouble if she left any of it out, or said anything good about the country. Her students have trouble with simple math, but they can go on and on about power imbalances and intersectionality and other goofy ideas like that.

"If the students are paying attention at all, what they hear is a drumbeat of how bad America is and that we should tear everything down and start over. That message appeals to youngsters who think destruction is exciting and have no idea how hard it is to build things up. It fuels the anger and resentment that we see in all the riots we've had.

"And even if a student did manage to get a good basic education and left school with a willingness to work, the government has been busy driving business away with tax increases and burdensome regulations. I know of several here in Laguna Beach that went bankrupt or closed down when the owners decided to move to Arizona or Texas—anywhere but California. And nothing takes their place. No one starts a business here any longer. The climate is hostile, toxic.

"So there aren't enough jobs for people. I never saw much unemployment in Laguna Beach in my life, but I do now. That saying 'Idle hands are the devil's workshop' is proven out here day in and day out. We get more crime—as you have experienced—and we get kids who are happy to live with their parents and spend their time playing computer games. We're in a downward spiral, and nobody in power cares to do anything about it because it would make them unpopular.

Jen thought for a second, then asked, "If things are that bad, Will, why don't the people vote out the politicians responsible and elect better ones?"

Will cleared his throat.

"Jen, you've got to understand that California became a one-party state a long time ago. The Democrats run it. Behind the Democrats are a bunch of wealthy interest groups that have things exactly the way they like them—the greens, the teachers, the public service unions, the lawyers. They've been bleeding the state dry without any thought about the future. On top of that, our elections are a joke."

"Your elections are a joke? Why do you say that, Will?"

"I came to that conclusion several years back when I had requested an absentee ballot. Well, no ballot came, and it was just a week before the election, so I inquired about it and was shocked to hear that I had already sent it in. *But I hadn't ever gotten it.* I knew what must have happened—it was intercepted and cast for the candidates the Democratic Party leaders wanted to win.

"Another funny thing—a guy I know checked and found out that in his precinct, *more votes were counted than there were registered voters.* The plain fact is that the election system is controlled by people who can manipulate it to stay in power."

"So you're saying that election fraud is real and not fake news," said Jen as Will took another bite of cheesecake.

He nodded and said, "I know quite a few people here who have concluded that voting is a sham—a pure waste of time. One guy got the numbers and found that 133 percent of the registered voters in his precinct had cast ballots in the last election. Another discovered that his mother, who passed ten years ago, had voted."

Jen had written columns declaring that vote fraud was a myth spread by angry conservatives. Maybe that wasn't true. She thought it was time to move on to another topic.

"Could I ask you about something you said earlier—about how you 'sort of patrol' that area in town. What did you mean by that, Will?"

"Glad you asked."

"I'm a member of a neighborhood group in town. We help each other however we're able to. I'm big and know how to use weapons from my days in the Navy, so I walk the area for an hour or two in the evenings. Sometimes I come across criminals and chase them off. It makes the people here a little less scared. Punks like those two who attacked you have been getting bolder and bolder in the last few years.

"Other people in our group help out in other ways. If someone has too many tomatoes from her plants, she lets others know they can come and get some. If someone needs a ride, say up to LAX, he asks if anyone can help, and often someone can. Ever since the state launched its war against independent contractors, it's been hard for many folks to find affordable transportation. We look for ways to help each other and often find them. It feels pretty good.

"Actually, my late wife started our group—we call it Free People of Laguna Beach—quite a few years ago. It began as an online community blog, and it caught on with lots of people. We're still online, but once a week, we get together in person since many of us old-timers still like talking to people face-to-face rather than on the internet or by text. We also have a little website.

"Our next meeting is tomorrow night. If you'd like to hear more about the real California and what ordinary folks think, you're welcome to join us. You might find some good information for your book."

Listening to ordinary people—that might just prove to be useful, Jen thought. After all, she had to admit, her sources of information were confined to a narrow spectrum of progressive writers.

"You know, Will, I *would* like to take you up on that."

"Great! Since you don't have a car, how about if I pick you up here at seven o'clock?"

"Yes, let's do it, Will. Now I'd like to ask you something else. You have a gun, but you're not with the police. Is it legal for you to have it after the big crackdown on firearms while Pat Farnsworth was president?"

Will grimaced.

"Pat Farnsworth—what a disaster she's been, first for the state and now the whole country. I could talk about her all day long."

Will looked around the restaurant. No one was close by, but he lowered his voice anyway.

"I bought that Sig Sauer years ago for protection. No matter what the courts think the Second Amendment means, I know that I have a right to protect myself and my property.

"Yes, I was legally obligated to sell it back to the government, but I decided not to. What I did instead was to sell an old .22 rifle that my dad bought for me when I was a teenager. It was only good for light hunting and hadn't been fired in thirty years or more, but I sold it and got my one hundred dollars.

"Lots of other people also sold guns they didn't have any need for. That made for impressive-looking piles of guns for the government to destroy, but it did nothing to get 'guns off the streets,' as Farnsworth kept saying. Actually, it only got some out of attics or basements.

"Farnsworth turned gun destruction into a photo-op meant to show that she was 'taking bold action against gun violence', but it was ridiculous. It was just theatrics, just mind manipulation for people who want to believe that government can make them safe. The truth was that all criminals kept the guns they use. And most of the law-abiding part of the population, like me, kept guns we need for protection. We keep them carefully hidden away. When I get home, my Sig goes into a desk drawer with a false bottom that one of my neighbors helped me create.

"So, no, the gun isn't legal, but I'm glad I have it."

Jen held Will's gaze.

"I have to say that I am too, Will."

After a few seconds of silence, Will continued.

"Well, despite Farnsworth's crusade against guns, crime has kept on getting worse. Gun control laws don't help, but politicians will never admit it. They use outrage over gun violence to get elected, but they can't stop it any more than King Canute could stop the tides."

Will took his last bite of cheesecake.

"So you don't like President Farnsworth's economic or gun policies, but don't you think that she did a lot for African-Americans with reparations and expanded diversity policies?" Jen asked.

Will closed his eyes and thought for a moment before answering.

"All right, let's start with reparations. Yes, terrible things were done to some of my ancestors, but the people who did them are long gone. I don't feel entitled to money taken from other Americans who had nothing to do with slavery or Jim Crow.

"As for the idea that reparations would somehow heal our imagined wounds, have the riots stopped? No. They're just as frequent as before the reparations began. The people who were demanding the payments now say that they're not enough. I think they're just scam artists who know how to profit from the anger they stir up. Reparations are a very bad idea. If Farnsworth thinks otherwise, it's because she is so out of touch with reality."

Jen had never heard anyone of any race say that reparations weren't at least a good concept. But here was a black veteran who said it was a terrible idea.

"Let me ask you this, Will—haven't you experienced racism in your life?"

Will refilled his coffee cup.

"Racism? Almost never. When I was in the Navy, there were a couple of jerks who seemed to look at me as if I were inferior because of my skin color. For months, I just ignored them. But one day, an officer overheard their stupid taunts. He was a white guy who must have been about six foot six. He glowers at the pair of them and says, 'Just what the hell is wrong with you morons? If I hear any more crap like that I'll make sure you get the worst duty on ship.' Then he turned to me and said, 'Sorry about that, Collier. Let me know if they ever bother you again.' They didn't.

"I haven't felt racism since then. The Navy was color blind. All that mattered was doing your job right. Funny thing though—I heard recently that the top brass has started including ridiculous books on what's called 'antiracism' on its Professional Reading Program. I hope the officers have the good sense to pay no attention to them.

"Real racism has mostly disappeared, so the people who are invested in racial antagonism have to make up new definitions and imaginary problems to keep people stirred up. Politicians often gain by making mountains out of molehills. Reparations is just one more example."

This man certainly was unpredictable. Jen sipped her coffee, waiting to hear what Will would say about diversity.

"Now, about diversity—well, I think it's the most overused word in English. Everyone is diverse. The two of us are diverse. We're different in many ways. But my twin brother and I are just as diverse. Our DNA is about the only thing we have in common. Heck, the two of us might have more in common than Nate and I do," Will said with a chuckle.

"Does Nate live here, too?"

"No, he moved to Nevada many years ago. He's a state senator, and I'm sorry to say that he's trying to do to Nevada what Pat Farnsworth did to California – ruin it with taxes, regulations, and cronyism. I've tried to reason with him, explaining that people do much better with voluntary cooperation than when the government steps in with force. But he tunes me out as if I were some ignorant kid.

"But getting back to diversity, I'll tell you what I think. Politicians like Farnsworth have been saying for decades that something must be done to make sure that we have diversity—meaning getting the right percentages of groups into every university and every occupation. In their minds, we don't really have equality until every group has the right amount of representation. That gives the government an unending job, which is what they want.

"I guess they assume that we 'underrepresented minorities' are terribly concerned that there aren't enough Black engineers or Hispanic doctors, or whatever. They think that our lives will be just fine once there are proper percentages of us in all those occupations. But guess what—*I couldn't care less about that.*

"Suppose I need a lawyer. I want one who is darned good, but where his ancestors came from is of no concern to me at all. I couldn't care less about the overall percentages of blacks in the legal profession—I just want a competent lawyer to handle my particular problem.

"If a black kid can get through law school and become a good lawyer, that's fine, but if he can't, then he ought to study something else he's better at and go into that field instead. When politicians and educators babble away about how dedicated they are to group equality, they're trying to show how virtuous they are. But their policies make things worse.

"In my opinion, the whole diversity thing is just leveraging a few Blacks—and whites—to get power. It's a distraction from dealing with real problems. The so-called progressive politicians keep pushing symbolic junk like reparations and diversity programs to make us minority voters think they're our friends, while all the time, they do nothing about real obstacles to our advancement. Our schools don't teach kids basic knowledge and skills. Licensing laws keep people from going into lots of jobs they could do because the requirements are ridiculously expensive. And it's awfully hard for poor people to start a business today. I don't think my dad could ever have gotten his laundry business off the ground in today's environment.

"This might sound cynical, but I think most politicians would have us remain poor and angry rather than successful and independent. They want us to look to them for salvation, not our own efforts."

Jen was stunned. She had always been certain that achieving group equality was a goal of underrepresented minority groups. How could a person of color say that this great, progressive project was doing no good at all? But one just had, and she had to admit that his argument made sense. And even more startling, Will saw the kinds of policies she had always thought were crucial to minority uplift as "symbolic junk" that impeded rather than helped them.

Jen realized that she had never experienced this before—*profound cognitive dissonance.*

Will finished his coffee and said, "Let me ask you, Jen—would it make any difference to you if there were more white people in the NBA, where they are underrepresented?"

"No, not at all."

"I didn't think so. And neither would it make any difference to me if there were more black players in the NHL. I think that things work out best if we allow each person to specialize in what he or she does best and give up on the idea that the government needs to engineer group equality."

Jen leaned back to collect her thoughts for a moment.

"Okay, I see your point, Will, but what about President Farnsworth's initiatives to close the racial wealth gap? The numbers are clear—whites own proportionately far more than people of color do. Wouldn't you say that she needed to address that?"

Will shook his head.

"All of her group equality rhetoric annoys me. As I see things, each person, no matter what his ancestry might be, ought to do the most he or she can to be as successful as possible. When I got a good paying job here, I wasn't thinking about any racial gap, I was using my talents to get ahead. People naturally do that. When I hear politicians talking about their plans for creating group equality, I know that they're just fishing for votes among people who want something for nothing."

Jen knew that she would have to think more about Will's amazing arguments for individualism later. Now it was time to change the subject.

"I'd like to know more about you, Will, if I might ask. You mentioned your late wife. Tell me about your family, please."

"Sure. I got married just after I left the Navy. My wife, Veronica, was a dental hygienist. We had three children. I mentioned our daughter in Walnut Creek and we also have two sons. One is a computer security consultant who lives in Tucson and the other is an electrical engineer in Dallas. Unfortunately, I lost Veronica during the Covid-19 pandemic."

"I'm very sorry to hear that, Will. Did she die of Covid?"

"No, she died of a brain tumor that went undiagnosed during the state's lockdown. She kept saying she had headaches, but by the time she was able to see a doctor, it was too late to do anything."

Will tried to go on, but his voice broke. He closed his eyes and swallowed hard before continuing.

"We couldn't even have a proper funeral."

Will stared down at his empty plate.

"I am so very sorry to hear that, Will. I can tell how much you miss her."

"Thanks, Jen. Since losing Veronica, I try to keep busy. I do Free People of Laguna Beach stuff. I maintain my old car. I see my kids and grandkids from time to time. I have a wonderful dog, a Labradoodle named Cody. And I'm trying to learn how to paint. I really enjoy those shows where someone shows how to paint a scene such as a lighthouse. We have endless beauty here in California and I enjoy the challenge of trying to capture it on canvas. Some of my neighbors think my work is pretty good," Will said with a smile.

"I would like to see your paintings, if I could, Will."

"I'd be happy to show them to you some time."

Jen looked around at the nearly empty restaurant.

"I really enjoyed this, Will. Again, thanks for saving me from those thugs. I think it's time for me to get some sleep, if I can, and for you to get back to Cody."

The two walked out of the restaurant.

"Do you have a card Will?" Jen asked when they arrived at the point where he would go out through the lobby, and she would head to her room.

"Yes, I think I do," he said, reaching for his wallet. Jen took a card out of her purse, and they exchanged them.

"Have a good night, Will. I look forward to seeing you and your Laguna Beach group tomorrow."

"Thanks, and you too, Jen."

Jen began the walk down the long corridor toward her suite. As she did, thoughts about the last few hours raced in her mind.

She had nearly been raped, or worse, in what she had assumed was a safe town. She probably owed her life to the timely intervention of an armed man at the last minute. Apparently, the stories about gun owners preventing crime—stories she had often mocked as 'fake news'—were true. Could it be that the gun laws she had always been certain were beneficial were, as Will had said, useless symbolism?

And was he right in saying that California was rotting from the roots? That Pat Farnsworth's years in power had not been glorious for the United States, but instead, as he thought, ruinous? She had always assumed that if any minority person criticized the government, it had to be because that person was a conservative plant—but that was not the case with Will.

What if her political convictions were all wrong?

A long-forgotten lesson from her high school journalism class came to mind: *above all, give your readers the facts.* The evening's events had reawakened that instinct.

Jen got into bed, but for more than an hour, she tossed and turned before finally falling asleep.

CHAPTER 6

Back to Vista del Oceano

Despite her poor night's sleep, Jen woke with the sun. She went to the fitness center and did a forty-five-minute workout on an elliptical, showered, then went to breakfast in the same restaurant where she and Will Collier had talked the previous evening.

She couldn't get last night's events out of her mind. She might have been raped or killed, but instead, she was unharmed due to the lucky intervention of an armed man. Unsettling as that was, the subsequent discussion with him had been even more so.

Will's outlook was so completely different, so unexpected, and so *reasonable*. He saw Pat Farnsworth as a scheming politician who had damaged California and the whole country, not as a visionary leader. *How did that fit in with her biography?*

While waiting for her omelet, she debated another question with herself—whether to mention the attack she had suffered in Laguna Beach to Pat, or not? She decided not to bring it up. What had happened to her would just be a distraction from the business at hand. *But if Will was right about rising crime resulting from government policies, it was relevant.*

Jen also debated this question—should she frame any questions for Pat differently? Will had given her grounds to question her belief that Pat Farnsworth's progressive leadership had been a great blessing for the nation.

There was another side to that question, a possibility she had not previously considered.

Whenever Jen had encountered criticism of Pat Farnsworth in the past, she had dismissed it as merely the product of right-wing billionaires, gun nuts, white supremacists, religious freaks, or some other component of the reactionary conspiracy to keep America stuck in the past. Her questions to Pat, on the rare times they touched on the fact that some Americans opposed her agenda, had been easy to answer: "Some people say this and how do you answer them?"

Did she dare to ask more probing questions and follow up if the former president's answer was a facile evasion?

Jen decided that she didn't have a strong enough foundation for going that way in their interview—that is, for treating Pat Farnsworth the way she treated Second Amendment advocates or people opposed to racial preferences in college admissions. She just didn't know what questions to ask to probe below the smooth surface of Pat's political rhetoric. Better not to venture there at all.

Moreover, she had a suspicion that doing any serious questioning might blow up the whole book project. She wasn't willing to risk that. After all, Pat had shown that she has a vindictive streak.

No, she would continue with Pat Farnsworth just as she had on the previous two days—with puffball questions and no pushback. Jen was going over the topics she wanted to cover when her food was served.

Right at ten, the familiar black SUV pulled up in front of the hotel. Jurgen greeted Jen stiffly and opened the door for her. When seated, Jen noticed that her hat still bore some dirt from its unplanned travels of the previous day. She brushed the dirt off and resolved never to let the wind blow it off again.

Jurgen got in and started the vehicle. At that point, Jen blurted out a question: "If I might ask, sir, are you armed?"

"Yes, of course, ma'am. The president's entire security detail is armed. You're perfectly safe here."

"Thank you—I'm glad to know that."

On the ride to *Vista del Oceano*, Jen made some notes about the topics she wanted to cover that day.

Upon arriving at the president's home, Jen was surprised to see Pat waiting outside, standing beside the tiled fountain.

"Good morning, Jen," she said. " I hope you had a good night's rest. I have been up for hours thinking about the situation in the Middle East—you've probably been following it on CNN. Anyway, I have made a practice of putting out tweets on a regular basis—so the country won't forget about me." Pat laughed at her little joke, so Jen had to follow suit.

"Here's what I just released: 'Israel's repeated acts of aggression against the Palestinian people call for United Nations sanctions!!' What do you think?"

Jen had never studied the conflicts in the Middle East and had paid scant attention to TV news for the last several days. But among progressive Democrats, it was a given that Israel was the bully in the region and was always responsible for trouble.

Jen wasn't about to question that belief, so she replied, "That nails it, Pat. And the people appreciate your comments on the important issues now that you're no longer in office."

Playing it safe.

The two walked through the house and out to the veranda. Even though there was no wind, Jen made a point of putting her purse on the brim of her hat. The aide brought out coffee and poured a cup for each of them. Jen was sure that another jolt of caffeine would do her some good.

"Well, what would you like to discuss this morning, Jen?"

"I thought we might begin with the way you took California's AB-5 law against 'the gig economy' and made it national policy."

"Yes, let's talk about that, Jen."

"I thought that AB-5 was among the best laws ever enacted in California. It was an essential step to stop the growth of, as we say, 'the gig economy.' If we are going to achieve an economy that works for everyone, we can't allow workers to fall through the cracks, lacking in all the protections we have legislated for employees. Those gig workers: drivers and writers, yoga instructors and interpreters, and so forth did not have the wage guarantees, union protection, safety regulations, and other benefits of being an employee. It simply wasn't right. It was *socially unjust* to allow companies to continue to abuse those workers by calling them independent contractors.

"That was a good law for California, and I knew it would also be a good law for the whole nation, so I pushed Congress hard to pass the Work Decency Act quickly. Both chambers heard testimony from disaffected workers such as the Uber drivers who said that couldn't make ends meet with their earnings. The bill was passed, and I signed it in a Rose Garden ceremony, surrounded by Americans who had been victimized by the gig economy.

"That was one of the first, and most important components of my drive to build a fair economy. I was delighted to have the support of many businesses and unions that saw the need for the national law."

"As I recall," Jen replied, "there was some opposition to the Work Decency Act. How did you deal with it?"

A pathetic question, but just what she expects.

Pat laughed. "We dealt with it the way all reactionary opposition should be dealt with—we ignored it. The House and Senate hearings only included witnesses in favor of the bill, and my press secretary dismissed the few reporters who tried asking snarly questions about its effect on some workers. That, I'm proud to say, was one of the hallmarks of my presidency. I never let the forces of reaction get any traction. I knew what was right, and once I'd made up my mind, I never let the naysayers get in my way.

"In the past, we often allowed right-wingers to water down or sidetrack legislation that the country needed, but I put an end to that.

"Of course, there is still more to do to end worker exploitation, but the Work Decency Act is a big step forward,"

Pat looked at Jen for agreement, but she was less enthusiastic about validating each of Pat's ideas than she had been at first. She knew that this law had caused a lot of hardship among people who had depended on part-time work. How could Pat know that the costs didn't outweigh the benefits?

"Yes, I can see how important your determination was," Jen replied blandly.

She thought for a moment, then said, "That leads into another topic I wanted to discuss, Pat, namely your thoughts on how the private sector fits into your vision for our future."

Pat brightened at that.

"Oh, there is nothing I'd rather talk about than my vision for America's future. I believe that America has a truly brilliant future now that we have taken the major steps needed to put our capitalistic, exploitative, racist past behind us. Of course, there is more to do, but we have undoubtedly turned the corner.

"With all our progressive reforms in place, America will bloom like a meadow of flowers, tended by caring gardeners who will ensure that every plant is equally watered and fertilized and that the weeds of greed and hostility can never take root. How do you like that analogy, Jen?"

Jen had been hearing those same frilly words for the last eight years and now found them rather childish. Couldn't Pat Farnsworth and her stable of presidential speechwriters come up with something better—something that wasn't an insult to an adult's intelligence?

"That certainly is an inspiring vision, Pat," Jen said flatly. "You're saying that since we are now more committed to equality, that will lead to greater prosperity."

"Well, Jen, our commitment isn't just to equality, but *equity*. What I mean is that we're striving for equal outcomes for all groups in society. Whites will no longer enjoy higher incomes than blacks; Asians will no longer have more college degrees than Hispanics, and so on.

"Once we have achieved equity, most Americans will be happier, even if they have somewhat less in the way of material things. Of course, I realize that capitalism, with its unequal rewards, did lead to a lot of production of stuff, but so what? It caused the less successful to feel excluded, looked down upon. In our new America, we will no longer have the unhappiness borne of social inequities. It's possible that we'll have less in the way of material goods, but we will share them equally, which is the key to social solidarity."

Jen wondered how much "sharing" was going on, as she sat on the veranda of the former president's magnificent home. She also wondered just how much less the country would have to share under Pat's flowery vision. Would people really be content with less? The rhetoric sounded nice, but you can't eat it.

Those strangely dissonant thoughts she kept to herself.

"Very good, Pat. We certainly must rid ourselves of social inequities and you've put us on that path. But what about private business? You told me that you come from a business family. If we are committed to social justice, can we continue to have capitalism at all?"

"Good question, Jen!"

"Capitalism might have been important in our early development, but socialism would be ideal now, with the government running the enterprises that produce goods and services. After all, it's obviously wasteful to have dozens of brands of toothpaste and deodorant. Capitalistic competition is so backward, so chaotic, so unsustainable. I hope that will come about under one of my successors. I know that President Barlow discreetly advocates a scientifically planned and administered economy. We are making progress, Jen!

"Certainly, in your lifetime and perhaps even in mine, I'm confident that we will see the transition away from the economics of personal profit to the economics of global interest. One of President Barlow's top advisors, Professor Edward House, has been working on the plans for it. The essential thing, though, is to rid Americans of the notion that there is anything good in conducting business for individual gain. We need government enterprises run by experts, under the oversight of socially minded regulators. We're all in this together, as I said many times in my speeches, and once we get everyone to see that, then we'll be able to enjoy true prosperity."

Pat looked as if she had just sung a dazzling aria and looked at Jen for her approval. Jen nodded with more enthusiasm than she really felt for her government-dominated economic vision. It didn't seem to be working out for California.

Pat continued, "For now, however, we have to live with private, for-profit businesses. They can provide for most of our needs, although we must draw some lines. Education, for instance, must be a purely governmental responsibility. Otherwise, we cannot be sure that children will be imbued with the proper values.

"But in their places, private business can be all right. We allow them to earn reasonable profits so long as they operate for the common good. And under my administration, we took steps to make certain that they are, *in fact*, doing so by creating the Business Social Responsibility Office in the Department of Commerce. It has mandated that all publicly traded companies have a diverse board of directors. The Office also has the authority to investigate complaints that any business is failing to live up to its social responsibilities, such as equitable treatment of workers maintaining reasonable prices.

"Naturally, the Office has hired people who have the correct outlook on business to investigate complaints and enforce its orders. Just last year, more than 25,000 businesses were fined for socially irresponsible conduct."

Jen remembered that Will had said something about businesses folding under pressure from zealous officials enforcing vague laws. Was Pat aware of the downside of her social responsibility campaign? Probably not.

Don't bring that up.

"That is a very substantial improvement, Pat. Businesses really have to watch themselves now. But what if some companies don't like operating under the Business Social Responsibility Office and want to leave the country?"

Or is that too edgy?

Pat smirked. "Well, they are free to go, but we also put in place a fifty percent exit tax on the assets of businesses that want to leave America. Only a very small number have done so—less than a hundred. Nobody misses them."

Jen pondered that for a moment, thinking that the people who had worked in those businesses might miss them.

"But Pat, isn't there some concern that business entrepreneurs and investment capital will avoid the U.S. and flock to other countries, particularly those that haven't yet adopted social responsibility regulations the way we have? How do we deal with that?"

"Good question. Yes, that is a major concern of mine. We have been working in the United Nations to promulgate global rules for business social responsibility. I'm optimistic that will happen under President Barlow. It would be unfair and destructive if we were to let some countries gain businesses just because they don't uphold international social responsibility concepts."

Jen was starting to feel a bit drowsy. She filled her cup with fresh coffee and drank.

"Of course, we need strong international standards. Now Pat, another topic we touched on the other day that I'd like to come back to is your unemployment policy. Let's go over your Guaranteed Government Job program."

"Very good idea, Jen. About half way through my first term in the White House, it became evident that the labor market was going through one of those phases when businesses just don't create enough jobs for all the people who want them, even though the government was doing a lot to stimulate the economy with large deficits."

Do I dare ask if those labor policies had anything to do with the decline in jobs? No. She might think I was being disloyal and provocative.

"Our economists explained that America's economy was in a 'mature' phase and therefore was running out of investment opportunities. To offset this, they recommended two things.

"The first policy was, as you mention, the Guaranteed Government Jobs program, the GGJ. All across America, there was a huge amount of socially beneficial work that needed to be done, and several million people who were unemployed. So the obvious thing was to set up government offices to hire people for work such as trash pickup, graffiti removal, planting grass and flowers along our highways, and so on.

"I had always thought that we should have a policy of guaranteed government employment since I view it as a basic right for people to have a decent job that pays a living wage. The rise in unemployment was just the catalyst we needed to get it enacted. Since we began the program, more than three million people have signed up for it. They are doing necessary, long-neglected work and being paid well for it.

"The other part of our attack on unemployment was to establish the Federal Financing Bank to fund approved new business ventures that met our criteria of being sustainable, green, and socially conscious. Within a year, the FFB had helped start new solar panel companies, recyclable battery companies, and other ventures that fit in with my goal of decarbonizing America. Thousands of people found good jobs working in those companies."

That jolted a memory in Jen. Within two years after the FFB had started, several companies it had loaned money to went bankrupt. Jen recalled a staff meeting at the *Post* where a young writer had brought that up and asked if he could do a story on the money that the FFB had sunk into those failed firms. The editor glared at him and said, "Young man, this paper is not interested in stories that cast doubt on progressive policies. You'd be wise to keep that in mind."

The FFB probably wasted a lot of money, but don't bring it up.

"Thanks for those details about your administration's battle against unemployment, Pat. Unemployment has remained very low for the last four years and that shows what good economic policies can accomplish."

Jen felt a yawn coming on but managed to stifle it. A bathroom break would help. She excused herself, walked into the house, and once in the bathroom splashed water on her face. She was very tired but didn't want to stop the day's interview just yet.

Returning to the table, Jen poured herself more coffee, then said, "How about if we talk about the rapid decline of the political opposition, Pat. Your first campaign was hotly contested, but since then the Republicans have gone into a tailspin. You've had majorities in Congress unlike anything since the time of FDR, and your re-election was overwhelming with over sixty-four percent of the vote and all but a few small states.

"Many political writers, including myself, have attributed that to the great popularity of your programs and the spreading realization among Americans that, to borrow a phrase, 'they have seen the future and it works.' I'd like to hear your thoughts on this."

Pat beamed.

"Oh, there is nothing I'd rather discuss than the way the country has embraced my vision of a safe, equitable, racially harmonious society with an economy based on sharing, free health care, and excellent education for all. Once voters got a taste for the kind of life I wanted for them, they turned their backs on all the opponents of progress."

Pat leaned closer to Jen and said in a low voice, "But just between us, the demise of political opposition was also part of my plan and it has worked to perfection."

That statement got Jen fully awake.

"Please do explain, Pat," she said, also leaning closer.

Pat drew a long breath and then said, "Ever since my college days, I have been certain that the opposition to social and economic reform in America was morally illegitimate. It was all a cover for greedy self-interest and foolish superstitions. The political opposition was merely an oozing pustule of ignorant racist, sexist, homophobic people with small minds—but sometimes with big wallets."

Jen had heard that standard recitation of the grounds for dismissing opponents of progressive thinking countless times. She had used it herself in her writings, and even in conversation with her sister. It was *easy*. But it did not apply to Will Collier. He wasn't ignorant or racist and his thoughts about the country's direction were not morally illegitimate.

She nodded as Pat continued, but she was starting to dislike this woman she had so revered.

"Throughout my political rise, I thought endlessly about ways to beat them down with the power of the government. When I was elected president and had the Senate under control, I knew it was time to strike.

"First, we passed the Protecting Your Most Precious Right Act, which asserted federal control over state conduct of elections. It was intended, of course, to change voting rules in ways that would enable us to maximize the number of votes for our candidates. The old Supreme Court would certainly have ruled it unconstitutional, but my new court declared it valid in an advisory opinion.

"The bill prevented rules such as requiring photo ID for voters and witnesses on absentee ballots while mandating same-day registration, early voting, and automatic registration of voters from federal welfare rolls. We were sure that with friendly election officials, those measures would provide us the advantage we needed in close states.

"And then, we had a great piece of good fortune with the Covid-19 pandemic. Many states adopted voting by mail, which meant that ballots would fall under the control of a friendly branch of the government—the Postal Service. Ballots cast by mail had always been a weak spot in the system that we took advantage of in areas where we had control—Chicago, for example—but now we had the opportunity to expand our control nationwide.

"We set up a secret task force devoted to figuring out how we could get enough ballots delivered to friendly hands to make sure we won close elections. Naturally, I was kept out of the details—plausible deniability, you know."

Jen nodded to Pat, but without enthusiasm.

"Another part of the plan was to use the IRS to go after big donors to the Republicans as well as those who supported right-wing think tanks and media outfits. Previous presidents did that, but my enemies list was much bigger, and we put far more manpower into it than my predecessors ever did. It took only a year or two for the message to spread that if you want to avoid trouble with the IRS, don't support anything on the Right.

"At the same time, we weaponized many other parts of the federal bureaucracy with instructions to go after businesses on our enemies list—the EPA, OSHA, the FBI, Department of Labor, and so on. A few employees objected to having their jobs turned into political warfare. They were immediately fired, of course. There was no room in my administration for weaklings.

"Money for Republican campaigns fell off and we saw several right-wing think tanks shut down." Pat snickered. "Oh, it was so delightful to see—the withering away of my opposition."

So it's not the case that Americans were won over to you, but that you used the power of the government to silence and intimidate the opposition. Is this any different from the tactics of tyrannical rulers throughout history?

"Our anti-hate speech law also helped immensely, as it was designed to. Who gets accused of hate-speech violations and is hauled before the Commission? Right-wingers, of course. We pushed through the law with the slogan, 'Free speech is good, but it must be used responsibly,' knowing that we would appoint the people who'd get to decide what speech was responsible and what speech wasn't.

"Given that the definitions of 'hate speech' and 'racism' had expanded to include almost anything, our commissioners had no trouble in upholding complaints about illegal publications. And given that we have an army of activists around the country who are eager to do their part by filing complaints against 'wrong thinkers' the goal of silencing most of the opposition was actually pretty easy—merely a matter of summoning the political will to do what should have been done long before.

"Another thing that helped, even though it wasn't exactly under our control, was the assist we got from the big social media firms by deplatforming and demonetizing right-wing voices. Their CEOs also assisted us by burying stories that could have hurt us in return for promises to use federal regulation against any competitors that might try enter their markets."

So that explains it. The big tech moguls weren't acting in the public interest when they suppressed news and books that helped conservatives; they wanted governmental favors in return. This is ugly.

"The right-wingers are finding it harder and harder to get their nasty little opinions out. And once we get the internet under full control, we'll be able to limit the opposition to covertly circulating paperback books and pamphlets with their backward ideas. Not many people read stuff like that anymore. We're moving close to stamping out opposition."

This is chilling. Pat Farnsworth's goals may have been good, but her methods are tyrannical.

"The icing on the cake," Pat continued, "was the way I was able to take control of the judiciary, starting with the Supreme Court, so that my enemies would no longer be able to hide behind the First Amendment.

"As I mentioned yesterday, my new Court crushed the old precedents holding that the government couldn't censor writings it disliked, and that sent a signal to right-wingers that their old 'freedom of speech' arguments wouldn't work any longer. There haven't been any First Amendment cases in years, showing that we have broken those people—*utterly broken them.*"

Those last words were spoken with a vehemence that Jen had not previously heard from Pat. It did not, however, surprise her.

"In all my years in office, Jen, nothing gave me more pleasure than watching those right-wing radio people and columnists hauled before the Commission and fined for their crimes. I thought of this as my own—but of course, you can't write this—*Final Solution.*

"The administrative proceedings of the Commission were not open to the public, but the Chair told me how one columnist I really despised, that know-it-all Frederick Douglass Garrison, had whined that his columns were merely informed argument that contained no hate at all. Nevertheless, she lowered the boom on him. The country sure doesn't miss his scribbling.

"Some of my fellow Democrats thought I was going too far and being unfair, but I didn't let them sway me. One of the things I remember best from my college days was a sociology professor's saying that 'the worst abuse of power is not to use it to accomplish something good.' How right she was. I had an historic opportunity to use power for good and did not waste it."

Pat took a deep breath and stared out at the ocean for a moment.

"I realize that there's more to be done, Jen. Dissidents are circulating inflammatory books and articles to undermine federal authority. Some are teaching their children on their own, in violation of the laws in many states against that. In her inaugural address, President Barlow promised to continue my unification program by doing more to root out the ideologies of darkness. As she does so, I believe that most of our remaining opponents will come around to see that they are fortunate to have been given the best country possible and will stop complaining about progressive control.

"Those who don't will have to be re-educated."

Pat sat back in her chair.

Jen chose her next words carefully.

"That is indeed a huge achievement, Pat. I was aware of the collapse of conservative opposition, but had never thought about all the moving parts in your *Final Solution* that brought it about."

Pat again leaned in close.

"Look, Jen—that might be an unfortunate phrase. We haven't imprisoned or killed anyone, of course. We're just using the government's power for good ends. So what if my methods didn't comport with the theories about government held by some long-dead white elitists back when they wrote the Constitution? Times have changed, right? I *couldn't* let some antique words on a piece of parchment keep me from achieving an historic breakthrough. *I just couldn't.*"

"Of course not, Pat. You couldn't."

For all of the propagandizing—that certainly was the correct word—the administration and its allies had done over the years, most Americans still thought that politicians needed to play by certain rules. Those rules included fair elections and free speech. Jen realized that, deep down, she was one of those Americans.

The former president had just told her that she had jettisoned those rules in order to cement permanent power for her party. What could she possibly write about that?

Clouds of doubt were forming in Jen's mind about this project. Pat Farnsworth's great presidency was starting to look more like a slide into tyranny.

After lunch, Jen and Pat talked for a while about environmental issues, but Jen found it increasingly hard to stay awake. At 2:00, she told Pat that she was getting one of her occasional migraine headaches and asked if she could be driven back to the Ritz to rest.

In truth, Jen never got headaches and just wanted to be well rested for the evening's meeting in Laguna Beach. She was eager to hear what those people had to say about their lives.

Even more, though, she was tiring of the woman she had almost worshipped.

CHAPTER 7

Meeting the Free People

Right at 7:00 p.m., Will picked up Jen in front of the Ritz.

"I hope you had a good day, Jen," he said as he opened the door for her. "You look well refreshed after last night."

"Thanks, Will. I needed a nap this afternoon, but now I'm eager to meet your neighborhood group."

"You'll like them. Our meetings are held in Agnes Mizawa's home. She has enough room for our usual group of fifteen to twenty people."

After a five-minute drive, Will parked his Oldsmobile on a quiet street. He and Jen walked to a tidy house with an abundance of flowers in planters around the porch. Will rang the bell, and in a moment, the door opened. Jen saw a diminutive Japanese woman with silver-gray hair.

"Good evening, Agnes. I would like you to meet Jennifer Van Arsdale. She is a writer from Washington who's gathering information for a book on the state of modern America, and decided to start by investigating our area. Last night she was attacked by a couple of thugs and luckily I happened along and chased the punks off with my gun. Afterwards, we had a long talk over coffee and I mentioned our group. She said that she would like to attend our meeting this evening to hear from some regular Californians."

Agnes turned to her and said, "Well, I'm very pleased to meet you, Jennifer. I think you might get some useful ideas from our group. Most of them are pretty outspoken about the way things have been going in America."

"I hope to learn a lot from them. Please call me Jen. And what do you do, Agnes?"

"I'm a half-way retired music teacher. For a long time, I have given piano lessons in my home. Sometimes I'd host student recitals here, which is why I have enough folding chairs for our meetings."

Ah, another music lover!

As the three walked into the house, Jen could see a baby grand piano and folding chairs arranged in a semi-circle. "I used to play the piano some. What kind of piano do you have?"

"It's a Kawai. I've had it for almost forty years and it's still going strong."

"And you said you're 'half-way retired'—what do you mean by that?"

Agnes looked up at the ceiling and shook her head.

"It's the stupidest thing. Several years ago, the state passed a law requiring that piano teachers had to be licensed. I'd been teaching piano for decades without a single complaint—except, of course, from students who thought I was too fussy about fingerings and tempo markings and so on.

"But it seems that some parent got upset with some piano teacher and griped to her state representative. Then that state rep, who must have been dying for some bill to introduce, drafted one to regulate piano teachers. Supposedly, the public needed to be protected from incompetent music teachers.

"That was just so typical of our government—somebody doesn't think something is perfect, so the state steps in to make things 'better.'

"But to get a license, you see, I'd have to go through a useless state-approved training course on the theory of music teaching, which would cost me several thousand dollars, plus I'd have to pay the state $150 each year to renew my license. I said, 'To hell with that.'

"I still give lessons, but I don't advertise and only deal with people I trust won't turn me in for unauthorized music teaching. I hope you don't mind being in the house of an outlaw."

Jen chuckled at that. "No, I don't mind at all, Agnes, and I agree—that *is* the stupidest thing. I'm sorry to hear that political busybodies have messed up your life."

Just then the bell rang and Agnes walked to the door to greet more guests.

By 7:30 p.m., the room was well filled with people. Only a couple of faces looked to be under sixty, Jen thought. There were rather more women than men, and the ethnic mixture was broad: some white, some black, some Asian, some Hispanic, and some that were hard to tell.

Will stood up and opened the meeting.

"I'm glad to see all of you here this evening. We have a guest with us. Her name is Jennifer Van Arsdale. We happened to meet last night under some unpleasant circumstances while I was walking the neighborhood. Fortunately, she wasn't harmed. Jen is a writer from Washington, and she's in the area to gather information for a book she plans to write—a book I understand that will be on conditions and trends in America today. She would like to hear from you.

"First, though, let's begin as we usually do with any news or problems you'd like to bring up."

An elderly woman dressed in black, seated across from Jen, raised her hand, and Will said, "Estelle Goldman, what's on your mind?"

In a grave voice, Estelle said, "A lot is on my mind, neighbors. You've probably heard about the latest outbreak of violence in the Middle East, with rocket attacks on Israeli cities and counter-strikes by Israeli defense forces. Apparently as a result of that, our synagogue was spray painted with swastikas last night and a message reading 'Finish the Holocaust.'"

"That's terribly disturbing, Estelle. I hadn't heard of such hatred against Jews in our area before."

"It has been building up in recent years. Once again, Jews are the targets of frustrated, ignorant people who seem to think that lashing out at us accomplishes something for them.

"And there's more. My grandson Ben, a senior at UCLA, has been suspended just days before final exams begin. What he did was simply to post a picture of himself with the Israeli flag on Facebook with the caption "Peaceful people should stand with Israel.'

"That post was seen by some other UCLA students who seem to live to create trouble for people they dislike, which includes those of us who support Israel. His post, Ben told me, was reported to the university's so-called Bias Response Team, which immediately met to recommend that he be suspended.

"The students claimed that Ben's post violated school standards because it somehow 'made them feel unsafe.' How can a mere picture with the Israeli flag make anyone feel unsafe? It's just their way of harassing people they regard as political enemies.

"Amazingly, the dean went along with this and ordered Ben's indefinite suspension. Now Ben won't be able to graduate on time—if ever—and his plans have been ruined. When Eliot called him to protest this ridiculous action, he replied that his hands were tied, right Eliot?"

The man seated next to Estelle, the only man in the group wearing a suit and tie, stood up and said, "Yes, and what I'm sure that really means is that he's afraid to cross the student zealots who can make life miserable for anyone who gets in their way.

"They could file a complaint with the Department of Education, saying that UCLA was not sufficiently attentive to their need for security, and that would mean months of headaches for the dean. Under federal regulations, officials are guilty until proven innocent when students accuse them of not caring enough about their safety.

"As for our grandson, if anyone has any ideas about what a sharp kid who doesn't have a college degree can do, please let us know."

Eliot sat down and the woman sitting next to Agnes spoke up.

"This seems to be a new trend—punishing students because they don't conform. Last year, my granddaughter was accepted at the University of Southern California, but one day in July, she was notified that her acceptance had been rescinded. The reason? She had put up a Facebook post saying, 'Black Lives Matter—but just as much as all others do.' The school told her that a committee had re-evaluated her acceptance in light of that 'troubling' view.

"It was so absurd that I thought she was kidding when she told me about it. But it was real. That made me wonder if USC has any confidence in its educational program if they only want students who already have what they regard as 'correct' opinions."

"Thank you, Beverly Sanders," said Will. "Matthew Abo has a similar story. Matt, why don't you tell our guest what happened to you."

A man with very dark skin stood up.

"Hello, Miss Van Arsdale, I am Matthew Abo. I'm originally from Nigeria. As a young man, I came to America to study, and eventually, I became a professor of sociology at UC Irvine. I had tenure, but the university fired me anyway during the campaign to repeal Proposition 209. That is the law the state enacted in 1996 to ban all kinds of racial preferences.

"During the campaign, I wrote a blog post in which I argued that we should keep the law as it was. My research had shown that minority students had actually done very well under the color-blind rule. More had graduated with valuable degrees, and I also found that high school students tried harder since they could not depend on preferences to get them into the top schools.

"But once that post was noticed by some of my colleagues, they organized a campaign against me. They claimed that my views were 'unacceptable' without ever saying why. The dean wrote me a letter informing me of my dismissal, saying that while he was in favor of academic freedom, it could not extend to statements that caused such controversy and thereby harmed the university."

"I'm shocked to hear that, Mr. Abo. You lost your tenured position simply over *a blog post*?"

"Yes, and I hated to lose my teaching job, Miss Van Arsdale, but in fact, I had been growing more and more dissatisfied for years. First, the administration told me that I was grading students too harshly by giving quite a few Cs and Ds and Fs when those grades were deserved. Many of the students complained, and the dean told me that it was insensitive of me to tell students who did poorly that they should put more effort into their studies. I had to play along and inflate grades.

"Then, I was told that my syllabus needed to include mention of my concern for student safety and 'inclusiveness'—as if the university was more about psychotherapy than teaching. And after that, everyone on the faculty was told to emphasize our commitment to 'anti-racism.' I just wanted to teach about sociology to students who wanted to learn, but the university had other priorities."

"It seems to me that the university has lost an excellent professor, Mr. Abo. Didn't anyone stand up for you?"

Abo shook his head sadly.

"A few of the serious students in the department sent the president a letter saying that I was one of the best teachers on campus because I challenged them to think, but that did no good. On the other hand, a professor in the Gender Studies

Department wrote a haiku—or as she called it, a 'bye-ku' that went:

Black man who acted white gone. Race traitors are not welcome. Students feel safe now.

"That got over ten thousand likes on Facebook."

"That's appalling. What have you been doing since the university fired you?"

He laughed mirthlessly, then said, "I am employed by Disneyland. Each day, I put on a Donald Duck costume and try to amuse people in the park."

Jen thought to herself that it spoke badly of American education if people could be suspended, de-admitted, and even fired merely for speaking their minds. She had occasionally heard conservatives complain that college campuses were becoming places of intolerance. Apparently, they had reason to do so.

Will again addressed the group. "Does anyone else have some news? If not, then I will let our guest take over."

Jen stood and looked around the room.

"Thanks, Will. As he said earlier, I am thinking about writing a book that looks at America today, and I want to hear from ordinary people like you. I think that you're often overlooked and taken for granted. I would like to know what you see as our—your—major problems. So, please let me know what is on your minds."

A man with Mexican features raised his hand and Will recognized him.

"Pablo Mendoza—what would you like to tell Miss Van Arsdale?"

"First, welcome to our group, Ma'am. Are you familiar with civil asset forfeiture? It's a huge problem for me and, I have heard, many other people across the U.S."

"No, Mr. Mendoza, I'm not familiar with it. Please explain it to me."

"Sure. I'm not a lawyer, but I'll explain it to you the way my lawyer explained it to me. There are laws in just about every state that allow government officials to seize and keep your property if they say that your property was someone how involved in criminal activity. If you're carrying lots of cash, for instance, police might say that you got it from drug trafficking. If your kid does something illegal with the car he borrowed from you, then they might take the car, saying that it was somehow 'guilty' of the crime.

"Whatever the reason, once they have taken the property, it's up to the owner to try to get it back. That means going through legal procedures where the owner has to prove his innocence. That's hard to do and very expensive for ordinary people. And if you don't manage to win your property back, the government gets to keep it, sell it, and keep the proceeds."

Jen jotted down *civil asset forfeiture* in her notebook.

"That's a horrible abuse, Mr. Mendoza. I take it that you have suffered from it."

"We certainly have. My wife and I—Anita is sorry she couldn't be here tonight, but her mother is sick and she's caring for her—have a bed and breakfast here. Or maybe I should say *had* a bed and breakfast, because almost two years ago, it was taken from us under civil asset forfeiture.

"What happened was that the police arrested some kids who were supposed to be working at their guaranteed government job dealing drugs on a part of our property that's screened off from view. A day after arresting the kids, the police came back and told us that they were taking our property under the civil asset forfeiture law. They said the property itself was 'guilty' of facilitating the crime, so they just took it from us. We had to leave our own property.

"Ever since, we have been fighting in the legal system to get it back. A group based near Washington is helping us in the battle, but the courts move very slowly, and the government puts up one roadblock after another, trying to wear us down. Even if we eventually get the property back, we have been without our livelihood for all this time, and the house is getting run down.

"When the government can just take your property without your having done anything wrong, nobody is safe."

Agnes, seated on her piano bench, spoke up. "Pablo, you should mention that Anita painted a target on your backs with that letter she had published in the *Orange County Register* accusing the police of corruption."

"That's right. Anita's letter probably had a lot to do with it. Our so-called public servants don't like being criticized and have their ways of getting revenge."

Jen took a deep breath.

"I had never heard about civil asset forfeiture before. I'm shocked that people can lose their property without being found guilty of anything. Is anyone trying to change or repeal that law?"

"Yes, but the police and prosecutors who benefit from civil asset forfeiture are a powerful lobbying group and the people who get victimized don't carry much clout with politicians. A bill to repeal the law keeps being introduced in the state legislature by a few members who can see how unfair and corrupting this is, but the bill is always defeated when law enforcement lobbyists say that they must have civil asset forfeiture to fight the drug war. That's enough for most politicians to say that we can't take away this law enforcement tool. Reform bills usually die, but I heard that New Mexico actually passed a good one."

"If I searched for other cases like yours, would I find more, Mr. Mendoza?"

"Yes, you would—all over the country."

"Thanks, Mr. Mendoza. You've identified a serious problem, just the kind of information I'm looking for. Now, what else is on your minds?"

A white-haired woman sitting next to Agnes raised her hand, and Jen motioned to her.

"I'm Lisa Burdette. I used to run a florist's shop in town, but the climate for business has gotten so terrible here that I had to close down several years ago. In this state, they treat business owners as just slightly better people than child molesters. We're hit with more and more taxes and costly regulations we must obey—if we can even understand them. Many are so vague that just about anything might be a violation.

"A few years ago, somebody complained to that Business Social Responsibility Office in Washington that I wasn't recycling all the material that I should. I thought I was but couldn't disprove the complaint and had to pay a one-thousand-dollar fine.

"Another time, I was investigated for discrimination. The grounds for that investigation was that I had posted a job ad that read 'Part-time employee needed for florist shop. Just need a friendly disposition.' The federal officials said that I wasn't acting with social responsibility because my ad implied discrimination against people who aren't friendly by nature. I was fined one thousand dollars again."

Enforcing social responsibility had seemed perfectly fine when Pat Farnsworth had spoken about it. This woman's experience put it in a different light.

"I say that whole thing is just a way for the government to hire a lot of little busybodies who think that business is bad and enjoy the power to harass us.

"Politicians talk all the time as if 'the business community' was some infinitely wealthy, powerful thing. But that's not true. Most businesses are small and the owners have to work awfully hard to scrape by. And now, with this excess profit tax, if we manage to have a good year, we have to fork over a third of what the government calls the excess to them. But if we have a losing year, the losses are all ours.

"On top of all that, they insist that we pay our employees more than they're worth and give them automatic raises. I guess that big chain stores can somehow survive it, but small businesses like mine can't.

"I used to have five employees. Nice people. I don't know what has become of them since I closed down. But with the new minimum wage and the raises, whether they've earned them or not, I simply couldn't afford go on.

"My husband left me enough to retire on, or at least that's what I used to think. Now, with inflation driving up the cost of everything so fast, I don't know. The future looks pretty grim to me. Laguna Beach has lots of closed businesses, but nobody has opened a new one in years.

"To me, it seems that government has become the enemy of Americans who simply want to be left alone."

"Thanks for speaking up, Lisa. That was very informative. Who else has something to say?"

A man with a neatly trimmed gray beard put up his hand, and Jen motioned to him.

"Hi, I'm Gordon Altschuler and I'd like to second what Lisa just said about inflation. Prices keep rocketing upward. The cost of electricity is crazy—when it's available—and a gallon of gas costs as much as an expensive bottle of champagne. I'm afraid that we're heading for the kind of runaway inflation that many other countries have experienced. Inflation cheats people who saved and it distorts business planning since future prices become very unpredictable. Inflation is very corrosive and it's getting rapidly worse It's one of our greatest problems."

"You're right, Mr. Altschuler—I know about inflation myself. Washington was always an expensive place to live, but in the last few years, costs have hit the roof. But let me ask you, what more do you think the government should do to stop inflation? Should the government get more strict in enforcing price controls? Should the businessmen behind the price increases be fined or put on trial?"

Altschuler rolled his eyes.

"I'm sorry, but inflation has nothing to do with greedy businesses. That's the lame excuse political leaders like to trot out anytime inflation soars. They say it's due to greedy businessmen—and women," Altschuler glanced at Lisa Burdette, "but the truth is that businesses are always trying to maximize their profits. Competition, however, works to keep prices on the whole level. In fact, during the late 1800s, when we supposedly suffered under the robber barons, prices steadily *declined.*

It's nonsense to say that all of a sudden, there is some outbreak of greed among businesses so that everyone can charge more. That's just what politicians say to pin the blame where it doesn't belong."

Jen leaned back in her chair, then asked the obvious question. "All right -- *who is to blame?*"

"I'm glad you asked, Ms. Van Arsdale. The blame rests with the politicians who keep creating more and more money to cover their insatiable appetite for spending.

"Throughout history, governments have often wanted to spend more than they collect in taxes, so they make up new, cheap money to cover the difference. In ancient Rome, they debased their silver coins to the point that, eventually, there was hardly any silver in them. Prices soared. In Weimar Germany, the government printed up huge quantities of paper money and added many zeroes to the notes. Prices soared. When anything becomes superabundant, the value of each unit of it necessarily falls. That's what inflation is—superabundant money losing its value.

"For more than thirty years, our government has been spending money wildly on a million things, most of which it shouldn't even spend one dollar on. That spending far exceeds the amount collected in taxes, but instead of printing up trillions of dollars in paper money, as in Germany, it borrows the difference. The interest on the national debt is now the biggest expense of the government, by the way.

"The Federal Reserve System then buys up most of the bonds the Treasury issues, which creates new money out of nothing. That money goes into the banking system to supposedly stimulate the economy. But it doesn't stimulate anything except the size of the government.

"To make matters worse, the government now pumps money that the Fed creates out of nothing directly into people's pockets through the Universal Basic Income program. The result of all of this is that we have more and more dollars to spend on a decreasing volume of goods. Prices can only go up. And when the politicians try to clamp down price increases with controls, that doesn't solve the problem but only causes shortages.

"When Pat Farnsworth tells the country that she's fighting inflation, she's conning us. Her uncontrolled federal spending is the very reason *why we have inflation.*

"You see, inflation is the price the people pay for a government that has become addicted to spending. Whenever any problem arises, count on our politicians to say that the answer is more spending. It makes them popular with those who receive the money, and the cost in lost purchasing power of the dollar is spread through the country is easily blamed on other people.

"The way things are going, the dollar will lose nearly all its value. Then the government will probably replace the old dollar with some new dollar, but that will merely be cosmetic; the new money will also lose its value. The underlying problem of excessive money creation will remain. Rampant inflation will undermine business and drive people into barter. To some extent, that's what we do in our group—we barter goods and services."

Jen had never doubted that inflation was due to business greed, but here was a knowledgeable man saying otherwise. What if he was right?

"That's interesting, Mr. Altschuler. You're saying that inflation is caused *by* the government, not a problem for government to solve. I must admit that I had never considered that. May I ask what you do and how you came to understand inflation that way?"

"Of course. For the last thirty-four years, I have owned a coin and stamp shop. And I learned to understand inflation by reading a lot about the history of money and credit. If you'd like, I could suggest a number of books that explain the truth about inflation—not the official, 'it's not our fault' disinformation. The place to start, I'd say, is with an economist named Murray Rothbard. Could I email you with some of his books about money, inflation, and government?"

"Yes, please do. And what do you think the solution is, Mr. Altschuler?"

"What we need is money that the government cannot create at will. If it can do that, it's almost inevitable that politicians will start trying to outbid each other in favors they promise voters to get and stay elected. As long as the U.S. had gold-backed money, we had stable prices and a small government. Since abandoning gold for dollars the government can make out of nothing, prices have kept going up, sometimes slowly but at other times rapidly. And worst of all, the government has grown to gargantuan size and has unbridled power over the people."

In the past, Jen would have snickered. She knew that some Americans were "gold bugs" who held to out-moded notions about money, and here she was talking with one. But maybe Mr. Altschuler was worth listening to.

"So you think the country should return to the gold standard?"

"Well, that's a necessary condition, but not a sufficient one. Gold, or any other commodity money, does keep prices stable and restrain the government, but if the population has a high percentage of people who expect free things from the government, gold will give way. That's what happened in the U.S. in the 1930s.

"Another great economist, Frederic Bastiat, once wrote that 'the state is the great fiction whereby everyone tries to live at the expense of everyone else.' That fiction is now embraced by most Americans. They've been conditioned by politicians like Pat Farnsworth to believe that they're entitled to a huge array of free things from the government.

"They never stop to think that government itself produces nothing and whatever it gives to them it must first take from others. That belief is like a plague, *a plague of the mind*. At this point, I don't think there is any cure for it."

Jen could think of nothing to say to that.

"Thanks for sharing your ideas, Mr. Altschuler."

Jen looked around the room.

"Now I'd like to toss out this question—what do you think former president Farnsworth's National Unity campaign accomplished? Is the country better off for having gotten rid of all the statues and monuments and so forth that caused so many Americans pain?"

Several hands went up at the same time.

"How about you first, sir," Jen said, pointing to a balding black man who sported a beard. "What's your name, please?"

"I'm Leonard Adcock, and I do tile work. I've got to say that I think her Unity Campaign was a colossal waste of money. Americans aren't any more united today than they were eight years ago when Patty Farnsworth started tearing things down.

"None of those statues and other things made the slightest bit of difference in my life. They didn't hurt me when they were up and I'm no better off now that they're gone. If anything I'm a bit worse off because I had to help pay for all those people who she appointed to decide what had to go and what could stay. That cost serious money that might have been used for something useful."

Again, not an answer that Jen was expecting.

"Thanks for your view, Mr. Adcock, but didn't the things we got rid of symbolize aspects of our history that African-Americans found disturbing?"

"Oh, sure, there are some of us who find it useful to whine about the distant past. It gets them attention and money. But almost all of us have better things to do than complain that some piece of stone and metal is ruining our lives. I don't think that any Japanese Americans go to pieces if they see a statue of FDR, who ordered their ancestors into internment camps—am I right, Agnes?"

Adcock turned to Agnes Mizawa, and she nodded.

"Everyone knows that many bad things have been done to many people throughout history, but it doesn't do any good to obsess over it. And tearing things down has done nothing at all to give us national unity. The people who demanded that monuments come down and buildings be renamed have just found new things to gripe about. We still have riots. We still have punks defacing synagogues. If anything, we're less united than ever.

"I say it was just a distraction from doing something about the real problems in America. All that Farnsworth's 'National Unity Campaign' accomplished was to empower and reward folks who get their kicks out of destroying things."

The woman who was sitting next to Jen put up her hand, and Jen nodded to her.

"I'm Susan Cho, and I have a little story about one of the destroyed monuments that you might find interesting. Up in Monterey, there was a monument to Commodore John Drake Sloat of the U.S. Navy. He was responsible for claiming California for the U.S. in 1846. A large, impressive stone monument honoring Sloat was built overlooking Monterey Bay in 1910.

"Naturally, it was listed for destruction because it supposedly glorified war and the taking of land that belonged to other people. So it was demolished, which took a lot of doing due to its size.

"The firm that did the demolition, however, never properly cleared the site. Chunks of rock and rubble were left all over. Kids liked playing there. But it also attracted rattlesnakes. One day a little boy was bitten and barely survived. Foolish ideas usually have bad results and this is sure a case of that."

"What a terrible story. Thanks for telling me about it, Susan. Anyone else on this subject?"

Will spoke up.

"I'd like to say that the demolition of Mount Rushmore really bothered me. I had thought that they at least wouldn't ruin a National Park, but I was wrong. I took my family there a long time ago and enjoyed the spectacle. So what if Washington and Jefferson owned slaves? They were still extremely important in our history; it never crossed our minds that the monument was somehow an endorsement of slavery, as its opponents said.

"I understand that if you go to Mount Rushmore these days, you can look up at the defaced mountain and listen to lectures from park rangers about how the United States mistreated the local natives. The National Park Service says they have 'contextualized' Mount Rushmore. Almost nobody goes there these days.

"Politicians like Pat Farnsworth love to get voters to focus on symbols and slogans instead of reality. Her great National Unity campaign was built on the premise that most Americans would get caught up in its symbols and slogans and forget that they were getting poorer and less free. Maybe it worked with some of the people, but not with me."

Jen nodded to Will.

"It seems that you folks don't think the National Unity Campaign actually did anything to unify the nation. The next thing I'd like to ask about is the new national anthem, but I have a hunch that you're not too keen on it, either—am I right?"

A woman sitting beside Estelle Goldman raised her hand, and Jen motioned to her.

"My name is Emily Stavrakis. I'd like to say that I think the Star Spangled Banner was a thrilling song and the new one—I can't even remember its name—is a damned bore. My dad took me to ball games when I was a kid and I liked singing the Star Spangled Banner before the opening pitch. The new anthem sounds like an apology. That's one of the reasons why Paul and I never go to games any more."

"Thank you, Emily," Jen said. Looking around the room, she continued, "What other things are on your minds?"

A dark-skinned man in a crisp white shirt raised his hand, and Jen motioned to him.

"Sir, what do you think is an important issue for the country these days?"

"Thank you. I am Ibrahim Khadimi. My neighbors know that I am a follower of Islam, but I want to say to the Goldmans how awful I feel at the news that their synagogue was desecrated. It is a very shameful thing to defile any place of worship and I pray that the culprits are caught and punished."

"We thank you for your kind thoughts, Ibrahim," said Estelle.

"The big problem I would like to discuss is trade—specifically how the country has become so hostile to it. For many years, I had a successful import business. I sold goods from around the world. I know that some of you purchased vases and rugs and chess sets and carvings and other items from me. But since President Farnsworth began imposing high tariffs on goods from countries she said were not trading fairly, much of my business is gone.

"Our former president, like so many before her, wanted to manage the economy to make it 'work for everyone,' as she put it. But her meddling in foreign trade has harmed many businesses like mine and, so far as I can tell, has helped no one. Lots of poorer people now have to pay quite a lot more to buy American. 'Buy American' is another one of those slogans Will mentioned—it sounds nice but distracts people from understanding what is really going on."

That reminded Jen of something her college economics professor had said: "Whether you're liberal or conservative, you should be in favor of free trade. Trade interferences have bad consequences for most people." Mr. Khadimi agreed.

"Thank you for that, Mr. Khadimi. While we're talking about the economy, what about unemployment? Anyone have something to say about that?"

A relatively young man—probably in his mid-forties, Jen figured—raised his hand. She pointed to him.

"Please tell me who you are and what you think about unemployment."

"I'm Mike Wunderlich. I run a tire and battery business. I'd like to say that I think the government is nuts. First, they pass a load of laws that make it more costly to hire a worker, and then after we have to let people go—or close down completely like Lisa—they come up with this brilliant idea of GGJ. Government Guaranteed Jobs. That's a total crock. The people who 'work' on them do little that useful. They pick up some trash along the roads and they paint over graffiti—which is back in a day or two—but other than that, I have never seen them do anything.

"Here's what I think. The government is wiping out jobs that actually produce value and then soaking up the unemployed with these ridiculous make-work jobs. And lots of young people never get a real job at all. They start off 'working' for the government and never even think of going into an actual job where you have to compete to get it and then produce if you want to keep it. I can't get any young people to work anymore. When the old guys retire, I don't know how I'll stay in business.

"Even worse, lots of those guys who don't have anything real to do get involved in crime. It's getting worse and worse around here."

Jen shot Will a glance.

"That makes sense, but what about the fact that the unemployment statistics say that it's very low?"

"Well, naturally the government tries to make itself look good. Unemployment only appears low because they don't count the millions of people who have signed up for GGJ as being unemployed, but they really are."

"Thanks for your thoughts on that, Mr. Wunderlich."

She looked around the room and asked, "Are there other problems you'd like to talk about?"

"What about the high cost of energy?" said a frail woman sitting next to Gordon Altschuler.

"Good. Let's talk about that. First, please tell me who you are."

"Carol McGinnis is my name. I'm a widow. Used to be a nurse. I have to make ends meet on a limited income. The government has raised my Social Security benefits, but that's not enough, especially with the sky-high cost we pay for electricity.

"I'm sure that Patty Farnsworth up in her mansion in the hills doesn't have to turn off the air conditioning when it's hot to save money, but I do. Her energy policies hurt lots of us Californians, and now they're doing the same to people all over the country—brownouts and blackouts have become normal. My brother in Louisiana tells me that he's had to cut back. He dreads the summer months when he can only afford to run the A/C for a few hours every day.

"Old Patty talked on and on about we had to follow her Green New Deal in order to save the planet. Well, I'm old enough to know that politicians use scare stories to get the people to hand them power. I've always been environmentally conscious—we all are. The U.S. is much cleaner than it used to be.

"But there was no need for her drastic 'decarbonization' crusade. I guess that's what her wealthy supporters wanted for some reason. They already have it made and can easily afford the cost of pretending to care about the rest of us.

"We've returned to a sort of feudalism," Carol continued, "where the high-and-mighty lived well and the common people just have to do what they're told and accept their lot in life. We ordinary people serve the government; it doesn't serve us. Instead of making progress, in many ways the U.S. is *regressing*."

California was supposed to be such a *progressive* state, thought Jen—all the brightest people said so. It was called 'the blue model' state. And yet all of these obviously sensible residents were saying that Pat Farnsworth had made their lives much worse.

Jen looked around the room and asked, "Who else would like to talk about what's going on in America and what you see for the future?"

A small, gray-haired man in a somewhat tattered sport coat raised his hand. Will spoke up first.

"Hi, Stan. I was hoping that you'd get into the conversation. Jen, this is Stan Zygalski, accompanied by his lovely wife, Ming. Stan is originally from Poland and often enlightens us on history and philosophy and other subjects. Just last week, he told us the fascinating story of how the Poles were able to defeat the Red Army, which Lenin thought would be able to march through Europe, sparking communist rebellions everywhere. Stan, why don't you tell our guest about your background."

"Glad to, Will."

"As Will just said, I was born in Poland. My father was a mathematics professor at Krakow University, the oldest in the country. We lived under communist rule and you had to watch what you said very carefully. My father thought his position was fairly safe, but one day he was accused—he said that he believed it was by a student he had failed on an examination—of harboring anti-Marxist thoughts. In fact, he did. He had secretly read many books and manuscripts that were critical of Marxism and was convinced that it was intellectual rubbish. He was very careful to keep his views secret, but perhaps he made some slip.

"Even though his teaching of mathematics was known to be excellent, once he knew that he was under suspicion, he assumed that eventually, the state would order the university to fire him—or something worse. Fortunately, he had some British and American contacts who were able to arrange for our family to escape from Poland in a freighter bound for Oslo. Had we been caught, my parents would probably have gone to prison for the rest of their lives and I can't imagine what would have become of me. But we made it to Norway and then on to the United States. I was ten at the time.

"Once we were in America, my father was able to get a faculty position teaching mathematics at a small college in Wisconsin, a state where there are lots of people who had come from Poland generations back. It was great. I studied accounting at the college, passed the CPA exam and found a job with an accounting firm in San Diego. Now I'm a senior partner and I can do most of my work online. Ming and I moved to Laguna Beach about nine years ago."

"So you have seen quite a bit of the world, Mr. Zygalski."

"That's right, but I haven't yet gone back to Poland. I hope to do so one day."

"What are your thoughts about the state of your adopted country? Do you see good trends or bad ones?"

"I used to be highly optimistic about America, but now I am very pessimistic."

"And why is that?"

Stan adjusted his glasses.

"My neighbors have already heard a lot from me on this, but since you've asked, Miss Van Arsdale, I will tell you. I'm afraid that the United States has taken a wrong turn from which it will not be able to return. The reason for that will, I think, surprise you."

Jen raised her eyebrows and said, "I'm eager to hear it."

"Sure. We have been undone by our extraordinary success in creating prosperity. That was predicted nearly a century ago by an Austrian economist named Joseph Schumpeter. He was one of the thinkers who made an impression on my father.

"Schumpeter's main argument was that capitalistic countries would eventually fail not because capitalism—by which I mean the system that emerges from private property and economic liberty—can't produce enough goods and services, but because it does so with such remarkable efficiency.

"He foresaw that in countries where free markets were allowed to work, there would be such an outpouring of productivity and ingenuity that eventually, there would be a large class of rich, bored people. Those people would grumble endlessly about the imperfections they saw in society, a society that had equipped them with the time, money, and verbal skills to start tearing it down."

That, Jen realized, was a good description of Pat Farnsworth.

"In America, Ms. Van Arsdale, capitalism has been dying the death of a thousand cuts from supposedly well-intentioned policies fostered by such people. Their policies impede production, obstruct innovation, reward idleness, and sow discontent. They divert resources away from wealth creation into wealth consumption, especially the sort of consumption they favor, like college degrees for everyone and subsidies for high culture.

"Pat Farnsworth and politicians like her never tire of dreaming up ways to make the country better—as they see it—with new mandates, prohibitions, taxes, subsidies. The more they 'accomplish,' the more the government grows, and the more people come to expect everything from it. And that, to use a currently popular word, is unsustainable.

"America used to bustle with ambitious, far-sighted people. I'm sure you've heard of Alexis de Tocqueville, who visited here in 1830 and wrote about the great energy of the people. What distinguished America from old Europe like his France was that Americans were perfectly free to work and pursue their own goals in life. They produced, invented, and traded without state-imposed constraints. Never before in history had there been such progress.

"As the nation prospered, a few people made huge fortunes, but ordinary men and women reaped most of the gains from their work. Neighbors helped each other when they were in need. Nobody expected anything from the government, which in any event had been given almost no authority to interfere in people's affairs. Americans focused their energy and ingenuity on improving their lives and their communities through voluntary efforts.

"But the country's great success in raising the standard of living in time started creating Schumpeter's intellectual agitators who found fault with the results of economic freedom—as they saw things, the rich were too rich and the poor were too poor. They insisted that the state must be given the power to improve matters by imposing their plans on the people.

"Those intellectuals were just fifth wheels as far as our free enterprise system was concerned. Their complaining was at first of no consequence, but in time their political candidates began winning with promises to create a more just society. Lots of Americans were, and continue to be gulled by utopian politicians who tell them that they will make things right—more equal, more safe, more clean, more unified—always by expanding the scope and power of the government."

Zygalski took a long breath. Jen stared at him thinking that she had never heard such strange, provocative ideas. But from what little she remembered hearing about her own Dutch ancestors in Michigan, his narrative made sense.

"I know it's trite to say, 'the world is divided into two kinds of people', but I believe that, and what I'm about to say in that regard is perfectly true. The world is divided into people who are happy to lead their own lives, peacefully interacting with others for mutual benefit, and people who want to dominate their fellow humans, dictating to them and taking from them.

"In short, there are *Makers* and there are *Takers*.

"In early America, the Takers had no traction. Our laws protected freedom and property. The government had no authority to redistribute wealth. As long as that was the case, the Takers were frustrated—they had no way of controlling people and taxing away their earnings.

"Unfortunately, the Takers began to get their way in the late 1800s. They worked for laws that infringed on contract and property rights—supposedly in the 'public interest.' They pushed for the income tax and the Federal Reserve system, both of which fueled the growth of government. They relished the wartime economic controls and free speech restrictions under Woodrow Wilson, which they believed pointed the way to the good society—one dominated by progressive intellectuals and political leaders.

"After the First World War—a tragedy due entirely to the arrogance and folly of governments—we had a respite under Harding and Coolidge, who dismantled the wartime regulations and returned us to constitutional governance. For a while, the Makers could go about their work unhindered.

"But the Depression put the Takers back in control. First Hoover, then Franklin Roosevelt tried all sorts of federal tinkering to restore prosperity in the country. For all their spending on government programs and restrictions on free enterprise, the nation continued to languish."

"Excuse me, Mr. Zygalski, but didn't the Depression happen because of the instability of capitalism? Wasn't Hoover a 'leave things to the free market' president whose inactivity allowed the Depression to deepen? And didn't FDR's New Deal get the country out of the Depression?"

"Respectfully, no, Ms. Van Arsdale. The Depression did not occur because of any instability in capitalism, but due to erratic policies of the Federal Reserve. Herbert Hoover was definitely not a laissez-faire president, but instead, one who believed that government actions were needed to get the economy back on course. His actions, however, just made things worse.

"Then, Roosevelt continued along the same path as Hoover, only he did much more in the way of federal activism, like destroying crops when millions were hungry and punishing businessmen for charging too little for their goods. Rather than restoring prosperity, FDR's regime prolonged the Depression with its relentless hostility to economic liberty.

"All of his meddlesome ideas had been cultivated for many years by people who wanted a vast, omnipotent government. I would assume that in school and college, you learned that Roosevelt was a great visionary whose ideas saved the country, right?"

Jen nodded to him.

"And you never heard that view challenged, right?"

Jen nodded again. Zygalski was correct about her education. FDR was one of the presidents she idolized, and she had never listened to anyone who criticized him. But she knew that she couldn't mount an argument against Zygalski, so she decided not to interrupt him.

"That shows how the Takers use the education system. It isn't so much for teaching knowledge and skills any more, but instead for implanting ideas in young minds that will incline them to question freedom and accept that the government has the solution to every problem. It's designed to create obedient citizens, not productive, independent ones."

"That's an interesting point. Please go on."

"Since the mid-1960s, the Takers have been constantly on the offensive. During some presidencies, they made only modest advances, but during others, they stormed ahead, bringing more and more of American life under their control. In the last eight years, their triumph has been solidified. Karl Marx, you surely know, famously wrote about class conflict, but he had the classes wrong. The contending classes are the Makers and the Takers.

"At present, the Takers have beaten the Makers into submission through their control of the government and its administrative apparatus. Intellectuals revile them. They're told that they didn't really build anything and whatever they produce belongs to society. Now, the Makers are starting to give up. Why work when the government will hand you UBI money? Why try to succeed in business when you'll face headaches and harassment from the government, with heavy taxes if you operate profitably?"

Zygalski stopped for a breath, and Jen asked him, "What do you think all of this portends for our future?"

"What it portends is that America will wind down, like a magnificent old clock whose mainspring has become almost completely unwound. The nation will keep losing its vitality as the Takers expand their control. Makers will quit in frustration or leave. Energetic immigrants will no longer come here.

"Our output of goods and services will keep declining, but at the same time, interest groups will demand larger shares of our shrinking pie. Conflicts will intensify and hatred will spread. Americans will live in fear of being ruined simply for saying the wrong thing to somebody or running afoul of some regulation they couldn't possibly have known about.

"Omnipotent government is a terrible thing, Ms. Van Arsdale. That, however, is precisely the legacy of President Farnsworth and her progressivism.

"Toward the end of his life, my father said, 'Stanislaus, I'm glad that we came to the United States, but life here is getting to be too much like it was under the communists in Poland.' If he were escaping from a tyranny today, he certainly wouldn't come here. He'd probably choose Estonia or Israel or Taiwan or one of the few other countries that have some regard for individual liberty. He'd go to a place where the incentives favor the Makers, not the Takers.

"When I first came here, I fit right in with everyone, despite my Polish accent. Now it feels as though the country has been conquered by a hostile alien force with a completely different set of values from mine and even a different language with bizarre concepts that defy comprehension.

"Worst of all, I feel deep animosity from the members of that force because I want no part of their domineering, destructive movement. They chatter endlessly about what a horrid nation we have been, but they never offer any constructive ideas for making things better. *America is being looted by those people. They are crushing its spirit.*

"And have you ever tried to have an argument with one of them? I used to frequently get into arguments online over matters of economics and history. But I learned that these 'progressive' people won't carry on a civil discussion. Once you clash with them, they resort to name-calling. They seem to believe that they win just through invective. I can't deal with people whose minds don't function because they are consumed with anger, so I stopped trying to argue with them."

Zygalski paused, and Jen saw her opening for another question.

"With all due respect, sir, it sounds like you reject democracy. After all, the people you say are ruining America were freely elected."

"No, Ms. Van Arsdale, I'm not against democracy, but I see it as a pretty frail governmental system. It worked reasonably well here for a long time, and that was because most of the people believed in liberty and weren't interested in using government to steal from or dictate to others. Democracy worked due to the moral character of the citizens, not because majority rule automatically produces wise leaders and sound laws.

"Once that character changed, however—once the Takers became a powerful political force—politicians who knew how to craft appealing messages teamed up with groups seeking government favors and the feeding frenzy was on. I fear that there's no stopping it now.

"Democracy doesn't guarantee that what's done will be for 'the public good.' Actually, democracy serves as an excellent cover for the Takers. They propagandize the populace that voting is their most precious freedom while they use government to deprive people of things that really matter—their liberty and property. For example, democracy gave us civil asset forfeiture, but that hardly makes it right."

"I see your point. Maybe democracy doesn't lead to good government. Let's say that you're right about our bleak future, Mr. Zygalski. Do you think that's what political leaders like Pat Farnsworth want? They're not *trying* to make us poorer, are they?"

He adjusted his glasses before speaking.

"Politicians like Farnsworth pay lip service to what they claim will be a beautiful future, but they don't really care if ordinary people will like it or not. What they care about—what they *crave*—is control. They're sure that they and their families will thrive on fat government salaries. It simply doesn't occur to them that their 'compassionate' laws and regulations could have disastrous long-run consequences. It's enough for them to revel in their good intentions, which the media constantly praise.

"Nor do many voters think about the long-term trajectory of the nation. Most take the current level of prosperity as a given. How many of the people who voted for Hugo Chavez in Venezuela thought that they would end up living in a wretched, totalitarian hell-hole?

"Like the poor Venezuelans, Americans are now figuring out that you can't eat ideology. Democracy has left them living less well than they did just a few years back. That's true for most of us in this room. It's true for many others in formerly vibrant coastal towns like Laguna Beach. It's true for far more people living in inland California and now it's true for millions all across America.

"We're in national decline, but on the rare occasions when our political leaders confront that fact, they say that it's actually a good thing because we've got to save the planet, and living more 'naturally' is good for us.

"I'm sorry to say it, but I'm certain that America peaked decades ago and will become steadily poorer. The very rich will remain so for a while, but the gap between them and the rest of the population will widen. That's an ironic result for politicians and intellectuals who always proclaim themselves friends of 'the little people' and profess their egalitarianism."

Zygalski took out a handkerchief to wipe his face, as Agnes' living room was getting quite warm.

"No doubt you have heard the phrase 'bread and circuses' with reference to the Roman Empire, Ms. Van Arsdale."

Jen nodded, although in truth she was not familiar with it.

"That's how the later emperors tried to keep the people content under their rule, with free food and free entertainment. President Farnsworth has gone back to that old playbook and updated it. No American goes hungry and everyone can be entertained round the clock—with frequent doses of government thought control. The Roman Empire rotted away from within and the same thing is happening to the United States."

Jen did know something about the fall of the Roman Empire and said, "But surely you aren't afraid that the U.S. will be invaded by barbarians coming from Canada or Mexico."

"No, we have our own home-grown barbarians and they have already ruined us."

At that, Zygalski leaned back in his chair.

"Thank you for listening to me, Ms. Van Arsdale."

"You're most welcome, Mr. Zygalski. I'm glad I listened—to all of you."

Will stood up and said, "Unless someone else has something to say, I think it's about time to wrap our meeting up."

All the other guests had gone, leaving Jen, Will, and Agnes.

"Thank you so much for your hospitality, Agnes, I can't remember when I have had such an intellectually stimulating evening."

"I am so glad to have met you, Jen and do hope you got some good material for your book."

They were about to head for the door when Jen noticed some music on the piano. She walked over and looked at it. Chopin's Nocturnes.

Jen turned to Agnes and asked, "Would you play one of the nocturnes? I have always loved them."

"I would be glad to. Which one would you like to hear?"

"How about Opus 27, number two—the one in D-flat."

Agnes sat down and played the piece. Jen closed her eyes, the better to savor Chopin's sublime music.

After Agnes had finished, Will and Jen said good night and walked to his Oldsmobile.

"Did you get some useful ideas for you book, Jen?"

"Yes, I did, Will, far more than I could have imagined. I learned more from your neighbors this evening than in the last twenty years."

As they pulled up in front of the Ritz-Carlton, Will's phone pinged. He read the text and muttered, "Oh my God," then turned to Jen. "It's from the Goldmans. Their synagogue is on fire."

Jen walked to her suite. She went to the balcony and stared out at the dark ocean, pondering what to do.

She had plenty of face-time material with Pat Farnsworth; another day wouldn't be very productive. What she really needed was time to think about everything she had just learned.

She decided to go home.

Jen picked up her phone and called Courtney Oliver.

"Mr. Oliver, this is Jennifer Van Arsdale. I hope this won't inconvenience you, but I think I have enough information from the president and something has come up in Washington. Could you arrange for me to fly back tomorrow?"

"That's quite all right," he replied. "How about if we pick you up at the hotel at noon for your flight back?"

"Thanks so much. This has been a most informative trip. Please explain to President Farnsworth that I regret cutting short our time together."

CHAPTER 8

Nicole Swensen

After her day of travel back from California, on Saturday morning, Jen was happy to go through her usual routine—Peloton ride, shower, a light breakfast. She was just about to open her computer when she heard her phone. Glancing at the screen, she could see that it was Maddy.

"Hey, sis," she answered.

"Back from California?"

"Yes, I got back last night."

"And how did it go?"

Jen decided not to tell Maddy about the attack in Laguna Beach.

"Well, Pat Farnsworth and I had many hours of productive and informative talks. I also happened to meet some local people who, truth to tell, weren't very enthusiastic about her."

"Oh, you mean that you ran into people with actual brains?"

Jen had expected a jab like that from Maddy, who was no friend of progressive politics. She often referred to her state as 'The People's Republic of Virginia' and said for some reason that her idea of a great president was Grover Cleveland.

"Well, Maddy, you'll be surprised to hear me say this, but those people did indeed have brains—just as Pat Farnsworth does. I learned a lot about her career and her presidency. I also learned that some Californians have a low opinion of her. They gave me much to think about."

"I'm surprised to hear you say that, Jen, pleasantly surprised. Feel like telling me more?"

"Sometime, Maddy—not just now."

"Okay but I'm dying to find out what has shaken your admiration of the great Pat Farnsworth. Have you gotten started on your book yet?"

"No, I still want to contact a few more people and then I'll have to do some serious thinking about how to approach the biography. You know that Schubert had his Unfinished Symphony; at this point, Jennifer Van Arsdale has her Unbegun Biography. I'm not worried, though. I have six months to get it written."

Maddy chuckled. "Very funny, Jen. Now here's why I'm calling. In case you've forgotten, today is Bonnie's third birthday and we're having a birthday dinner and cake for her. Want to come over around five? And if you could stay with her this evening, that would save Josh and me the cost of a babysitter when we go to the concert this evening."

"Sounds good to me, Maddy. I'll be there."

Jen checked the time. It was just after 10:00. Would it be all right to call someone in Eastern time on a Saturday morning? The first person on Greg's list was in Ohio and in their email exchange, the woman had said that Saturday morning would be fine. She decided to make the call.

Jen punched in Professor Nicole Swensen's number in an area code she was sure she had never before called—741.

A soft woman's voice promptly answered. "This is Nicole Swensen. How may I help you?"

"Good morning, Professor Swensen. This is Jennifer Van Arsdale. You'll recall that I recently contacted you by email. I would appreciate any time you can give me to talk about your former Dartmouth classmate and now our former president, Patricia Farnsworth."

"Oh, certainly. I'm now retired and have lots of time to talk. And please call me Nicole."

"Very good, Nicole. And I'm Jen. I'll start out with this question. You were Pat Farnsworth's roommate at Dartmouth and no doubt got to know her well. What did you think of her election and presidency?"

Jen could hear Nicole draw a long breath before answering.

"Yes, I did know her well and to be honest, I was horrified at her election. And her presidency was even worse than I had assumed it would be."

Jen paused for a moment, surprised by Nicole's sharp answer. *Didn't anyone like Pat Farnsworth*?

"*Horrified*, you say? Would you please elaborate on that?"

"Sure. At Dartmouth, Pat Farnsworth thought she was the greatest thing on campus—and wanted everyone else to know it. The fact of the matter is that those of us who knew Pat Farnsworth were put off by her bossy, know-it-all attitude. You couldn't have a polite disagreement with her. Oh no. She was right about everything and everything had to be her way. Eventually I learned to keep my mouth shut around her since even what you'd think was a safe topic might set her off. Terrible temper, especially if she's been drinking."

"I appreciate your frankness, Nicole. Please continue."

"I could go on all day about her. Here's one of many incidents I remember. The first week we were rooming together, the student paper ran an editorial arguing that it was time for the U.S. to pay reparations for slavery. She was talking on and on about how it was time for the country to pay reparations and how that would start the process of healing historical wounds. She apparently figured that I would agree at some point, but when I didn't, she finally stopped talking and gave me a puzzled look, then said, 'You don't look too enthused, Nicole. Maybe you think that fifty-billion-dollar figure is too low.'"

Nicole cleared her throat, then continued.

"I answered Pat that I didn't think *any* amount was proper. At that, she fumed and said, 'How can you be against something for your own people?'"

"*Your own people?*"

"Yes. I'm Black. Mostly Black, anyway. But I have never thought of myself as part of any group. I grew up Nicole Jones, not 'African-American Nicole Jones.' My father was a major league baseball player who made a pretty good living and went into the car business after he retired.

"He told my brothers and me that we'd be happiest if we forgot about race and got along with the great majority of Americans who didn't care about our ancestry, but just what kind of people we were. 'Make the most of your abilities and you'll all do just fine,' he often told us. Late in his life, he said to me, 'Nicky, there are a lot of people of all colors who will try to get you to help push terrible ideas just because of your beautiful skin. Don't let them.'"

She took a moment before continuing.

"Anyway, I said to Pat that I couldn't see why the rest of America owed me anything and that instead of healing, reparations would merely become a new source of animosity."

"And how did she respond to that?"

"She just looked at me bitterly for a minute and then said something like, 'America will never make any progress if people like you won't stand up and demand change.' She never made an *argument* that I was wrong, but slammed her books down on her bed and stormed out of the room."

So here is another African-American who disagrees with Pat Farnsworth's ideas for healing the country. I thought I knew how they thought but was very wrong.

"That's very revealing, Nicole. You found Pat Farnsworth to be highly opinionated and temperamental. But what was she like as a student?"

"Well, I thought she wasn't much of a *student* because her life seemed utterly consumed by political causes. I recall a day when several of us girls were talking about courses we were thinking about for the next semester. Pat said she was eager to take a Women's Studies course with some professor who had written a book that was high on the *New York Times* bestseller list. Another student said she wanted to take that course too because the professor's theories were so key to the transformation of society.

"That student then asked me—Pat didn't deign to speak to me any longer—if I was going to take that course, and I said that I wasn't because I wanted courses based on actual knowledge rather than flighty opinions. Besides, I added, courses like that were known to be easy as long as you didn't express any contrary thoughts. I was in college for intellectual challenges and didn't care to waste time on courses that had no real content. Pat mostly took courses like that women's studies course—light on knowledge, heavy on grievances."

"Still, Pat did extremely well at Dartmouth, didn't she, Nicole? She graduated *magna cum laude*, right?"

"That is true, Jen, but she managed that by avoiding all the hard courses. I also suspected that she paid people to write a lot of papers that she got As on. It was fairly easy to skate by in courses like Women's Studies and Theories of Literature, unlike STEM courses."

"What was your major, Nicole?"

"I majored in biology and later got my Ph.D. in it."

"That's very impressive. What else can you tell me about Pat Farnsworth?"

"Here's another revealing story about her. Someone on the faculty had scheduled a guest speaker to give a talk on campus—an economist, I believe. I distinctly remember his topic, which was discrimination in pro sports. Since my dad had been a baseball player, I was very interested.

"The trouble was that Pat and her allies had heard from some national activist group that the speaker's views were racist, so she organized a campaign to protest him. She and her pals posted signs around campus that read, 'No Racists at Dartmouth!' with an ugly drawing of the man. I didn't think there was any reason to call him that and wanted to hear what he had to say.

"Immediately after the speaker was introduced, Pat and her bunch began shouting at him and chanting their 'No Racists' chant. Several times, the professor who had introduced him asked for quiet so he could speak and each time, he'd say just a word or two before he was interrupted.

"Finally, after about fifteen minutes of that, someone from the administration showed up and asked that the protesters remain quiet until after the speaker had given his talk. They just booed him, but at this point the rest of the students—about one hundred of us—started to shout back at the protesters, 'Shut up or go away!' They went away, chanting as they walked out."

"So then the talk went ahead?" Jen asked.

"It did, and I thought the man made perfect sense. His argument was that competition to make money in pro sports was the big reason why the color barrier eroded as quickly as it did. There was nothing remotely racist about his talk and I couldn't see why anyone would call him that. I also couldn't see why college students at Dartmouth or anywhere else would feel the need to protest someone before listening to what he had to say. It seemed childish, but I certainly didn't want to provoke another fight with Pat by asking why she was so ready to smear someone she didn't know.

"That wasn't the end of it, though. The next day, there was a letter in the campus paper signed by The Committee to Defend Dartmouth Against Racism, claiming that the school administration had violated their rights in asking for quiet so a 'known racist' could be heard. What that showed me was that Pat had no respect for the rules of common decency. I couldn't resist sending in my own letter to the paper, asking why a few students thought they were entitled to decide what others should be allowed to hear. I then summarized the speaker's case that market competition undercut racial discrimination and challenged anyone to prove him wrong. My letter got no response, of course."

Jen realized that Nicole had just given her the other side of an incident that Pat had made to sound noble. But in her telling, there was nothing noble about it, just immature rudeness and intolerance. Still, she wanted to hunt for some redeeming virtue in Pat's conduct.

"I agree that shouting speakers down is pretty bad, Nicole, but couldn't it be that Pat Farnsworth's activism, even if overly zealous, sprang from her passionate commitment to helping minorities?"

Nicole answered immediately.

"I don't think so. It was all theatrics. And passion, even if real, is no excuse for rudeness. Besides, it doesn't help anyone to tear down the rules of civilization."

"That is a good point," Jen admitted.

Pat Farnsworth was looking less and less admirable. The woman that most of America, including Jennifer Van Arsdale, had been led to believe was a high-minded advocate of social justice was just a bully who had to have her own way. Jen wanted to know more.

"Can you think of any other college incidents involving Pat Farnsworth that Americans would find illuminating?"

"Certainly. One day she was on the phone when I came into the room, talking to her father about a professor who she was angry at. She was ranting about how he was so unfair and unreasonable because he had given her a D on a paper and wouldn't change the grade, despite all her complaining. This was apparently one course she had figured would be a snap and turned out otherwise.

"She was saying to her father, 'Couldn't you have your attorney threaten to sue the college if they don't get rid of Professor Richberg?' After he had answered in the negative, Pat said, 'What do you mean that's not what the law is for?' and hung up."

Oh, yes—this must be the one Dartmouth professor who Pat had said "disappointed" her.

"She wanted her dad to get a professor fired? What had he done?"

"I also wanted to know that—and, fortunately, I knew a guy who was also taking that course—it was on Political Theory, I think. I asked him if he could fill me in on this juicy incident.

"He told me that after the students had submitted their first papers, Professor Richberg had said to the class, 'After reading your papers, I couldn't help but think that most of you were just trying to write what you thought I wanted to hear—not doing your own analysis. College should be about original thinking, not merely regurgitating popular opinions, even if they're mine. So I am going to give you a new assignment, one that is meant to expand your minds. I want you to read a famous book by a right-leaning author and write a paper making the strongest argument you can in favor of his stance regarding the proper role of government."

"Would you happen to remember the title or author of that book, Nicole?"

"The title, I think, was *The Road to Serfdom*. I have heard it mentioned a few times over the years. I understand that it's an important work and that the author won a Nobel Prize."

"Thanks. Please tell me more."

"Sure. When Richberg returned those new papers, he had given Pat a D with the comment 'Your work here shows almost no familiarity with the book and no attempt at all to do the assignment of presenting an argument in favor of the author's position.' She showed it to my friend, hissing, 'That old Jew bastard can't do this to me.'

"Now, I knew nothing about the subject, but wasn't surprised to hear that Pat had chosen to ignore the assignment since it called for trying to understand what someone looking at the world from a different perspective was saying. It must have upset her feelings of self-righteousness to have to acknowledge that people she wanted to have as enemies—like the econ professor who gave the talk about sports—might have some good ideas. This really underscored a key point about Pat—she wasn't actually interested in education, but just wanted to be with people who'd validate her beliefs."

"Do you know what happened to the professor who had gotten Pat so angry?"

"Pat griped to the dean about him, saying he was biased. But Professor Richberg wasn't fired or even reprimanded. Back then, Dartmouth at least sort of stood up for faculty members who were under fire for upsetting students. I think it was even seen as an aspect of academic freedom to grade students on the quality of their work. Pat dropped the class to protect her GPA. That mattered more to her than the chance to learn from an esteemed scholar."

"You don't have much good to say about her, do you, Nicole?"

"No, I certainly don't. She's a bossy, vindictive, know-it-all. Just the opposite of the kind of person you want to hold the highest office in the land. And here's something else about her that I can't stand. *She never admits that anything is her fault.* Eight years as president, and I don't think she ever accepted responsibility or admitted to having made a mistake. I wasn't surprised since I saw that character flaw in her when we were in college.

"We had been rooming together for a few weeks, and one day I got back to the room after my morning classes. Pat was still in bed. When I pulled out my desk chair, the noise woke her up. After glancing at the clock, she yelled, 'Why didn't you wake me up? It's after eleven, and now I've missed a test in English.'

"So she stays out drinking, sleeps through a class, and says it's my fault! Nothing is ever her fault, whether it's failing to getting up on time or the inflation that's ravaging the economy or increasing crime or anything else. By the way, she liked putting away the booze and had some nasty hangovers. When she's in that condition, look out. We called her Pat the Brat behind her back."

"I'm glad to know that about her. You've given me a lot of insight into the real Pat Farnsworth. Now if you don't mind, I'd like to know more about *you.*"

"Okay. As I said, I'm a recently retired college professor. For more than forty years, I taught biology at Ohio University. Not *Ohio State* in Columbus. *Ohio U.* is a state university in Athens, in the southeast corner of the state. I chaired the Biology Department for ten years before my involuntary retirement last year."

"Involuntary—how so?"

Nicole drew a long breath.

"That had its roots when a new president was selected about three years ago, Derek Elizondo, who insisted on being called 'Doctor' because of his advanced education degree. There was a lot of eye-rolling over that.

"Anyway, he was eager to transform Ohio U. into a 'social justice' institution so it would more completely address the country's various crises. He called it 'Our Deep Commitment' and what it entailed was for all courses to focus as much as possible on 'equity and fairness.' It also mandated anti-bias training for all faculty members.

"The one measurable metric was that Elizondo was determined for OU to become the state's leading school in the percentage of students who graduated. He wanted that to be his mark—just processing the most degrees.

"His administration didn't discuss any aspect of the plan with the faculty. After its unveiling, the provost informed all of us that we had a week to submit our plans for compliance with Our Deep Commitment.

"I was one of the few senior faculty members who protested against this imperious *diktat*. We drafted a letter to the whole OU community, including the trustees, arguing that what *Doctor* Elizondo was calling for was inconsistent with the purpose of a university, an attack on academic freedom, and a sure-fire way to devalue degrees from OU, since making a high graduation percentage our goal would mean lowering our already dubious academic standards.

"Furthermore, we pointed out that because faculty members were supposed to have control over their courses, the 'social justice issues' mandate undermined our authority. And just what are the 'social justice issues' in biology, anyway? When I asked that question, all I got was silence.

"I loved teaching and knew I was sticking my neck out, but I was tenured, was the departmental chair, and so I wasn't really worried about the repercussions of challenging the president's plan. But repercussions there were. Those of us who signed the letter were told to either withdraw our signatures and apologize for our misbehavior or else face loss of all our benefits, offices, library access, and so on."

"They can do that to tenured professors?" Jen asked.

"Yes, they can. The old academic norms have been washed away by the commitment of activist educators to transform our colleges and universities to suit their visions.

"The thing that probably bothered me the most about this atrocious plan was the threat to have monitors sit in on all our classes to make sure that we were obediently working in the obligatory 'social justice' material. That was intolerable, but I knew that Elizondo and his underlings could make life miserable for us if they chose to. Just ignoring him and going about your teaching was unfortunately not an option.

"In fact, part of his plan was a new bureaucracy -- hilariously called the Office of Academic Excellence -- that we knew would be staffed with his loyalists, just itching for chances to ferret out any suspected deviants. The Soviet Union used to run its universities the same way – conform or get out."

Poland, too, Jen thought, recalling Stan Zygalski's story.

"I no longer wanted to teach at a school where academic freedom was obviously a thing of the past, so I resigned. Funny that the professor who was given my old place is a white guy who, students have often told me, is lousy at explaining biological concepts in class and spends as little time with them as possible. Of course, he's happy to go along with the new president's political obsession – a poor teacher but a good team player.

"The result is that OU now has less of the diversity they always say is so vital and also a less capable teaching force. The administration does, however, have the ideological homogeneity it wants. I would say that shows where their priorities are."

That circumstance—ousting a black woman—who was good at teaching in favor of a less competent white guy—bothered Jen. She cut in to say, "It seems to me, Nicole, that the leadership at OU doesn't have the mindset of serious educators."

"No, they definitely don't. The sad fact is that you find few serious-minded educators in American education any longer. From kindergarten through grad school, they are now mostly *apparatchiks* who like the good pay and job security in schools and colleges. With them, education runs a distant second, if even that."

"That's really disturbing."

"It certainly is. Here is another instance that speaks volumes about what has become of higher education in this country. A young adjunct math professor was in the faculty lounge when he noticed a pile of literature promoting Critical Race Theory. He wrote on a whiteboard 'Someone should take out the garbage' with an arrow pointing to the literature. Another faculty member saw that and reported him to the administration.

"After a so-called investigation, the school decided to fire him because he did not exemplify its values. I would say that if the school's values exclude the freedom to criticize pet beliefs like CRT, then that's the problem, not the professor.

"Now, that's bad—firing a math professor because his political beliefs weren't correct—but it's still worse when you think about the cost to the university of defending against the subsequent litigation. Elizondo doesn't mind wasting money on lawyers just so he can pretend to be the perfect model of a modern university president."

"*That* really is bad, Nicole. Makes you wonder how people like your Doctor Elizondo get picked for university presidencies," Jen replied.

"Now, I'd like to switch gears and ask about your thoughts on one of Pat Farnsworth's signature achievements—her Free College Program."

"I'm glad you asked about that, Jen. I think that Free College was one of the worst of her many awful initiatives."

Even though Nicole disliked Pat and her policies, Jen had anticipated a more favorable reaction from a college professor on the free college program. *Certainly*, it was good to allow more people to get their degrees—and yet she thought otherwise."

"Okay. Why do you say that, Nicole?"

Jen heard her take a long breath.

"Before Farnsworth's so-called free college, the U.S. was already luring huge numbers of poorly prepared and weakly motivated students into college with easy financial aid. In my opinion, it was a tremendous mistake for the government ever to have begun subsidizing college with loans and grants. The inflow of money enabled colleges to spend more, mostly on non-educational things, and to raise tuition. And then the politicians would say, 'Look—now we need to increase student aid to keep college affordable.'

"The government's easy student aid programs started bringing into college a lot of weak, poorly motivated students. Many of them could hardly read and write at what used to be expected of middle-school kids back when I was that age. Colleges soon began aggressively marketing themselves to maximize enrollments. Within a few years, the notion that getting a degree was an essential step toward a successful life had taken hold.

"I could see the change. While a small percentage of OU students really wanted to learn about biology or math or economics or other disciplines, more and more of them just wanted four years of the 'college experience'—plenty of beer and circus, as one author entitled a book on what had gone wrong with higher education.

"Those students wanted college to be mostly fun with as little of the drudgery of learning as possible. They'd come in as freshmen knowing nothing and, eventually, most of them would graduate, knowing hardly anymore. While in school, they would pile up a big load of debt, which many later struggled to repay—and frequently couldn't repay. The idea that college was a great 'investment' simply wasn't true.

"The former system was wasteful in the extreme, but Farnsworth's free college program made it worse. After it was enacted, our colleges and universities did enroll more students, but nearly all of them were even weaker than the bad students we had previously. We scraped the bottom of the barrel, so to speak.

"Naturally, college leaders wanted to keep all the students happy so the money faucet from the government would remain on full. To accomplish that, they added new courses with negligible academic value and pathetically low standards that would appeal to those kids. They also pressured the faculty to make their courses more 'user friendly', which meant that we had to water down the content and inflate our grades."

Jen remembered hearing the same thing from Matthew Abo at the Free People meeting.

"As for grade inflation, I did as little as I thought I could get away with, since I believe that it is no favor to students to be told that they did A work when in fact they had learned almost nothing. Incidentally, that's the problem with most of our high schools—they go through the motions of education but pay no attention to the bad results. Students are led to believe that they're excellent when they're actually poorly educated.

"And now, thanks to Farnsworth's Free College program, we're pretending to educate more students than ever but are deriving less educational value. The country pays for an increasingly dysfunctional higher education system while the education establishment grows fatter. Only a country as wealthy as America could afford such a wasteful system.

"And one more thing—people take far more interest in things when they have some financial stake in them. Cars people own are better cared for than rentals. By the same token, when people are paying their own money for education, they put more effort into the coursework. Make it all free and most students slack off. That was my experience at OU after it became 'free.' Most of the students got their credits by taking popular, easy courses, and they avoided the remaining difficult ones."

Nicole paused and Jen saw her opening to ask a question that had been on her mind.

"But isn't it true that more jobs than ever require a college degree, Nicky? If we didn't try to put more of our young people through college, wouldn't many of them face unemployment?"

Nicole gave a derisive laugh.

"Well, that's the argument the president used to sell her plan, but it's utter nonsense."

"Utter nonsense?"

"Yes, utter nonsense. There really aren't many jobs that an individual with a decent high school education couldn't possibly learn to do. When you hear that an employer 'requires' applicants to have college degrees, that almost never means that the work is so demanding that only someone who had graduated from college could have the knowledge essential to perform it.

"What it means instead is that the employer does not want to bother interviewing anyone who hasn't been to college. It's a legal way of discriminating against people who they assume would be harder to train than a college grad would be. The college degree is used as a screening mechanism, not a knowledge requirement.

"Employers can screen out workers who don't have college degrees because there is such a glut of workers with them. The result is *credential inflation*. Just as we have grade inflation in college, we have credential inflation in the workplace. It compels people to spend lots of time and money to get college degrees they don't want or need so they can have a chance at anything other than menial work.

"Do you see the problem, Jen? The more people we put through college, the more years of education employers demand."

"I had never thought of that," Jen said quietly.

"Very few Americans have."

"An OU colleague of mine dedicated most of his career to studying the economics of higher education and wrote several books explaining why we are 'going broke by degree' as he put it. But nobody in power listened to him or any of the other writers who have argued that America has badly oversold higher education. The truth is that the huge expansion of the college sector since the mid-1960s has happened for political reasons and not because of any educational necessity."

"Nicole, I remember covering the congressional hearings on the Free College bill, but don't recall that anyone addressed the point you just made about causing credential inflation and lowering academic standards. That ought to have been considered. It's a crucial point."

"Right. Well, that colleague I just mentioned was asked to testify on the bill, but he later told me that it was an exercise in futility. He went to Washington with his testimony ready for the House Education and the Workforce Committee hearings.

"He sat in the hearing room for hours, listening to one person after another testify in favor of the bill, speaking in clichés about how great an advance it would be for America to have free college and how it would enable us to surpass other nations as if college degrees were like Olympic gold medals. Those were the witnesses the majority of Democrats wanted the press and the public to hear.

"Late in the day, the committee chairman announced that he was sorry there wouldn't be time for the remaining witnesses to speak, but they could leave copies of their prepared testimony for committee members to read. Of course, they never did. Congressional hearings aren't a search for truth but merely a way to help justify decisions that have already been made. But you're a Washington writer. You know that."

She was right again.

"All right, but won't free college help us to keep up internationally?"

"No, that's another silly slogan she used. Simply graduating the most people with college credentials – and master's and doctorates – doesn't mean that those individuals will make *productive use* of any of their education.

"The countries that do the best economically are those that make the best use of their resources. Pouring resources into formal education for people who don't want or need it is wasteful and lowers our prosperity".

"You sound more like an economist than a biologist, Nicole," Jen said with a chuckle.

"Thanks, but it's not hard to grasp basic economics. My colleague's books made it pretty easy.

"I'm afraid we are now stuck with a policy that wastes time and money trying to educate people who don't need college degrees, but just some basic workplace skills. If our K-12 schools worked half way decently, students would have that."

"I take your point, Nicole, but let me ask one more question about higher education. Isn't it a good thing that we are getting more minority students into college? At least Pat Farnsworth helped to close the racial achievement gap, didn't she?"

Jen heard a loud sigh from Nicole.

"Sorry, but that's another of those ridiculous slogans you hear from politicians. Sure, we haul more minority kids into college and slap degrees on some of them, but few have learned anything of value. You've probably heard that expression, 'the soft bigotry of low expectations.' Well, it happens to be true. Those kids are treated as though they were fragile figurines. I'm glad I got my education before it became fashionable for whites to worry about us blacks."

Jen collected her thoughts for a moment, then decided to ask a question she had posed at the Free People meeting.

"Thanks, Nicole. I can see why you don't think Pat Farnsworth's higher education policy was good. But how about the other big changes she made for the country? For instance, her program for cleansing the U.S. of offensive statues, names of unworthy people on buildings, hurtful public art, and so on. As a person of color, wouldn't you agree that that was necessary and beneficial?"

Nicole gave a snort before answering.

"A 'person of color? I have to say that I don't like being grouped that way as if my ancestry somehow determines how I think about the world.

"There is no reason – no science – behind the tendency so many Americans have of lumping people into groups instead of treating them as unique individuals. The Nazis, you know, used to claim that Jews were a group who thought differently from Aryans. Hitler denounced what he called 'liberal Jewish science' and most Germans went along with that.

"But speaking just for myself, I will say that I thought the whole program was and is pointless. It was simply a distraction from dealing with America's actual problems.

"The idea that people were somehow oppressed by the metal in a statue or the name on a building is ludicrous. But we paid big salaries to a lot of government officials to identify all of the statues, public art, names on buildings and of sports teams that they said could be offensive, and then we paid other people to tear down the bad statues, put new names on buildings, repaint murals, and so on.

"The squandering of money continues to this day. The Commission is still at work, hunting down tinier and tinier things to destroy or rename in their quest for purity. Being from Washington, you know, I'm sure that the most important thing for any bureaucracy is self-perpetuation."

"Yes, I guess that's so," Jen muttered.

"And exactly how is the country any better off now? Statues and names and murals never prevented anyone from getting a good education, finding a job, or raising a family. Now that Pat Farnsworth has 'cleansed America,' none of that is any easier. Nothing has really changed and the complainers have found new excuses for their failures and new reasons to be angry.

"One of the worst things about politicians in general and especially Pat Farnsworth is how they gain power by getting the people fixated on symbols so they'll forget about reality."

Jen had also heard that point in Laguna Beach.

"But didn't you feel bad about statues of Confederate generals and buildings named after people who owned slaves?"

"No, Jen. I am perfectly aware that human history had lots of terrible things in it. Of course slavery was terrible, but it's long gone, at least in the U.S. And let's be adults—a statue of someone who owned slaves hundreds of years ago no more endorses slavery than does a statue of Andrew Jackson endorse the mistreatment of American Indians. We can talk about the bad parts of our history without a destructive rampage that accomplishes nothing."

Jen knew that a national columnist had lost his job for suggesting, in milder tones, that the National Commission was useless. Here she was on the phone with an African-American who emphatically agreed.

"Thanks for sharing your views, Nicole. Now if you don't mind, I'm interested in finding out a bit more about your family."

"Okay—ask anything."

"What does your husband do?"

"He's a tax lawyer. At least, the president's big tax overhaul has been a boon for him. He has more work than ever, particularly small business people who the IRS is targeting because they're suspected of favoring Republicans or supporting groups that oppose our leviathan state."

"And your children?"

"We have two sons. The older, Warren, was very studious, and from a young age, wanted to become an engineer. He earned his engineering degree in three years, I'm proud to say. He's now a senior manager in a large firm.

"Sometimes he complains to me that students coming out of college these days with engineering degrees often lack the basic knowledge that engineering grads used to have. He blames that on the push for making all the STEM majors more diverse.

"He once said to me, 'Mom, if a bridge collapses, are people going to say it's okay because the engineering profession now has more women than it used to?' I told him that, unfortunately, almost no one would think to blame it on the obsession with group representation that has swept our education system.

"Warren's younger brother, Paul, is just as smart, but he wasn't interested in college. What did interest him were boats. He was fascinated with boats.

"When he was a high school senior, he cold-shouldered our pleas for him to look at colleges. On his own, he found an entry-level job with a boat building company on the eastern shore of Maryland. He did very well and stayed with the company. He was happy, but my husband and I had to deal with people who would look at us as though we were failures when we told them that Paul didn't go to college. What he learned from work was boat design and eventually started his own firm."

"That's quite a story. How is Paul doing these days?"

"I'm sad to say that his company is struggling to stay in business. Pat Farnsworth's tax overhaul was good for my husband, but it drove a stake into the heart of the boat industry. Far fewer people can afford them now, between the new luxury goods taxes and the high cost of fuel. He thinks that he'll be bankrupt by the end of the year."

"I'm very sorry to hear that, Nicole. Paul must be pretty upset over that turn of events."

"Oh, he's way beyond upset, Jen. He's talking about moving to another country where business ambition is still rewarded."

Thinking it was time to wrap this up, Jen asked, "How about giving me a summary of your impressions of Pat Farnsworth?"

"All right. I would say that she is arrogant and intolerant, way too sure of her own ideas, way too aggressive in pushing them, and unable to see that they are wreaking disaster on the country. I fear that my children and grandchildren will have a poor, bleak future unless we can somehow undo the presidency of Pat Farnsworth. We've got to ditch her utopian dreams and turn America back into a land of freedom and opportunity. You can quote me, but I'm sure that would sink your book.

"But I'm very pessimistic about turning America around. Those of us who study biological processes know that organisms can fight off many infections and return to good health. But we also know that once a disease has gotten to a certain stage, the body cannot fight it off and succumbs to it. I'm afraid that Pat Farnsworth has pushed the country past that point of no return. We will linger for a long time, but will never regain good health."

"Thank you, Nicole. That is a vey sobering assessment of your old roommate. I have greatly enjoyed our conversation."

"And I have as well. Please call me at any time if you come up with more questions."

Jen sat back in her chair to think.

Everyone she had spoken to thus far had a highly negative impression of Pat Farnsworth. Far from leading the United States into the 'radiant future' she always to talk about, these people thought she had done enormous, even irreparable harm.

Jen was getting less and less enthused about writing the hagiographic biography she had initially meant to.

But at a deeper level, she was wondering if her own beliefs might be mistaken. Ever since her days at Oberlin, she had been utterly certain that America was a broken land that could only be fixed by the power of the government. She had dismissed any and all who disagreed with that as foolish and ill-educated.

Having now spoken with quite a few people who disagreed and who were neither foolish nor ill-educated, Jen was wracked with doubt.

Allegro walked over and rubbed against her ankle. Pensively, Jen stroked her head.

Maybe the next person on her list, a professor at Stanford Law School, would have something favorable to say about Pat and restore her confidence that Progressivism was the right path forward.

But it was too early to call California, so she puttered around the house with a symphony that Schubert had completed, his Ninth, playing in the background.

CHAPTER 9

Alexander Oistrakh

Jen made a grilled cheese sandwich for lunch, watered her plants, and then decided it was time to call the next person on Greg Stein's list. She picked up her phone and called Professor Alexander Oistrakh, who had been one of President Farnsworth's professors at Stanford Law School.

"Hello. This is Alexander Oistrakh."

"Good morning, Professor Oistrakh. This is Jennifer Van Arsdale. I emailed you yesterday about the book I'm researching on your former student, President Farnsworth. You said that you'd have time to talk about her with me today. Is this a good time?"

"Oh, yes, Ms. Van Arsdale. I will be glad to answer your questions if I can. She was a student of mine more than forty years ago, but I will help you as much as I can.

"Just one thing, though—I'm in chemotherapy and might get too tired to continue. If so, we'll need to continue our talk at a later time."

"I'm so very sorry to hear that, professor. My mother went through chemo a long time ago, and I know how terribly it drained her. Do let me know if you feel that you need to stop our interview.

"Now, I'd like to begin with the courses she took from you and what you thought of her as a student."

Oistrakh cleared his throat.

"Pat Farnsworth took two courses with me—Constitutional Law in her first year and my seminar on the First Amendment in her third.

"In Con Law, I must say, she made very little impression on me. That was a large section with around one hundred and twenty students. One thing I remember was that I called on her for a response to a question I always like to ask students regarding the Supreme Court's jurisdiction in *Marbury v. Madison*. I picked a name at random, and it was Patricia Farnsworth. 'How would you answer, Miss Farnsworth?' I asked.

"No one answered, and I scanned around the classroom. I soon noticed a woman in the second row, looking very chagrined. Staring at her, I asked, 'Are you Patricia Farnsworth? We're waiting to hear from you.' She stammered, 'Yes, I am, Professor Oistrakh, but I am sorry to say that I haven't gotten around to reading the case yet, so I don't have an answer to your question.'

"To that, I replied, 'Miss Farnsworth, if you come to class, you ought to be prepared on the cases.'

"That was my only impression of her in Con Law. Rarely did she venture any questions or comments in class. I couldn't say what her grade was. I suppose you could ask the university, but I don't think you'd get anywhere. Stanford has sealed off her records, I understand."

"Thank you, professor—that's useful information about the Con Law course. Now what about the seminar you mentioned?"

Jen heard Oistrakh take a long breath.

"Actually, I have quite a few memories of her in the seminar—none of them favorable, I must say.

"There were about twenty students in it. Pat Farnsworth was very outspoken, but every time she spoke up, she displayed unsettling malice towards the idea behind the First Amendment—that speech and publishing should be free of government control. Her contrary notion was that speech should be put under government regulation so that it will be 'balanced'—as if the clash of ideas were a sports contest that had to have a referee.

"She also expressed support for legislation against 'hate speech'—a hopelessly vague concept that other students argued would lead to the extinction of freedom of speech and press.

"Pat Farnsworth's ideas led to some sharp exchanges with other students who argued that the Founders were right to keep the government on the sidelines with regard to speech, the press, and religion. In those arguments, she would invariably respond with some childish attack on the supposed motives of those students without responding to their points.

"I thought it amazing that a student at Stanford Law would resort to *ad hominem* arguments against those who disagreed with her. She actually seemed to believe that she 'won' such arguments. It was embarrassing. You'd expect high school kids to know that arguments have to be met with counter-arguments, not with anger, but Pat Farnsworth did so repeatedly.

"Once, I objected to a particularly nasty personal response she'd made to a student who had disagreed with her, and her reply went something like, 'I was exposing his biases, and according to Professor Emily Chalmers, the exposure of biases is actually the highest form of argument.'

"That told me a lot. Pat was evidently one of that new breed of law students who preferred to take the tendentious, ideologically driven courses that the law school was offering more and more. The kinds of courses that a law school professor I knew characterized as 'bad sociology, not law'. Professor Chalmers taught one of them, and it had very little to do with the law and everything to do with validating the leftist preconceptions of students who wanted to use law school as their springboard for an activist career."

Professor Swensen had identified the same bellicose, anti-intellectual streak in Pat.

Oistrakh continued, "Getting back to my seminar, for the major assignment, I had the students write a paper on any First Amendment controversy, past or present. Pat Farnsworth submitted a paper defending the government's crackdown on freedom of speech during World War I. She said that the government should prohibit speech that undermined its objectives, and not just during war.

"Her paper was appallingly weak. Not only was poorly written, at a level you might expect from a college sophomore, but it ignored all views contrary to hers. Lawyers need to learn how to marshal *arguments*, but it seemed that she didn't think she needed to bother with that. Furthermore, I was certain that large portions of the paper had been plagiarized from recent books and law review articles saying that the First Amendment was 'out of date.'

"At the time, I was thinking, 'This is a dangerous idea, but it could never take root in the United States,' but as we know, it has taken root, thanks to Pat Farnsworth and her Anti-Hate Speech Act. She has dragged us back to the time of Star Chamber proceedings against dissidents."

So—another person who didn't like America's first female president.

"Would I be correct to think she didn't do well in the seminar, professor?"

Oistrakh snorted.

"I gave her paper a generous D, commenting that it was just an extended rant rather than a legal argument. She was taking the course Pass/Fail and I strongly considered giving her a Fail, but decided not to because I was sure she would protest to the dean. Then I would have to waste a lot of time defending myself before an administrative tribunal. Giving her an honest grade just wasn't worth the trouble, so she got a 'Pass.' "

"Obviously you didn't think that the former president was a good law student."

"Certainly not. In fact I have often wondered if she had someone else take the LSAT for her. The people on the admissions committee who thought she was good material for the law school should hang their heads in shame."

"Professor, how about if we move on to Pat Farnsworth's political career? I would like to hear your thoughts on topics besides the First Amendment."

"I'd be glad to talk about her political career, which first came to my attention when she was California's attorney general. Let's cover that first.

"Pat Farnsworth served as the state's attorney general for four years. During that time, she worked ceaselessly to promote herself. Her tenure as AG was all about raising her public profile in order to run for governor. She brought many cases against the governor's political opponents and many more against people who had run afoul of one of the state's countless regulations, such as homeschooling parents and unlicensed cosmetologists.

"On the other hand, her office turned a blind eye to evidence of electoral fraud and contractors making illegal kickbacks to powerful Democrats. We'd had AGs who had weaponized their office before, but Pat Farnsworth took the cake.

"As I mentioned before, as a law student, she seemed to dislike the idea of blind justice and neutral rules of law, and as AG, she showed that day in and day out. There was one standard of justice for those who supported the Democratic Party and a different one for everyone else.

"Bad as her time as Attorney General was, her two terms as governor were much worse. She pushed the 'green' agenda to the maximum. Among the many consequences of that, California now has *by far* the highest electricity rates in the country and the least reliable delivery system.

"Of course, her green backers think that's good. It gratifies their egos to believe they're saviors of the Earth, but for millions of our poorer residents—and it's a sad fact that we have the highest rate of poverty in the United States—those rates are devastating. Pat Farnsworth couldn't care less about people who have to swelter in the heat because they can't afford air conditioning any longer. Too bad there are never any stories in the media about them."

Jen knew that was true. It was an unwritten rule of journalism that you never pointed out the bad effects of progressive policies.

"And as governor," Oistrakh continued, "she eliminated charter schools and homeschooling is now so heavily regulated that few parents dare to do it any longer. Naturally, the teacher's unions loved her and put tremendous amounts of money and manpower into her campaigns, but our public schools are for the most part lousy and with less competition, have gotten lousier.

"Students get regular lessons designed to make them to grow up to be supporters of omnipotent government—such as the intellectually dishonest '1619 Curriculum'—but most of them never even master the basics of English and math. Governor Farnsworth kept saying that her goal was a quality education for all children. What she really wanted, though, was *politicized* education."

Will Collier had said the exact same thing about public schools in California.

"Lots of youngsters who could have made something of themselves with a solid education are now becoming either wards of the state or predators upon society because there is no escaping the twelve-year sentence of our failing public schools.

"Farnsworth also pushed through a huge tax increase on high-income Californians, saying that it was time for the rich to pay their fair share. That line drew cheers from the throngs of people who are consumed by envy, but the result has been a great exodus of small to medium-sized businesses and of professionals. I know doctors who have moved to Texas and lawyers who have moved to Tennessee.

"Very few people try to start businesses here anymore. Entrepreneurs don't come to California these days—nor for that matter the rest of the U.S. Her 'fair' tax has sapped the vitality of the state, mainly to the detriment of poorer people who now have little opportunity for advancement.

"On top of all that, she disappointed even many fellow Democrats when she blocked reform of the state's civil asset forfeiture laws."

"I know something about that, professor. I recently heard about a terrible civil asset forfeiture case in Laguna Beach."

"I'm not surprised. They pop up all over the country. Do you know that if the owner can't work through the legal maze that's set up to make it hard for people to get their 'forfeited' property back, the government gets to sell it and the proceeds go into the police budget? So you can see why law enforcement likes it.

"They say, 'We need civil asset forfeiture to fight the war on drugs,' but it hardly ever puts a dent in drug trafficking. The people who get hurt by it are usually innocent people who get snared. Civil asset forfeiture is such a blatant affront to due process of law that a coalition of people from all parts of the political spectrum formed to push for civil asset reform in California.

"But if you think Pat Farnsworth's professed concern for 'the little guy' would put her on that coalition's side, think again. She made certain that the bill died in committee. Why? Because she wanted support from police unions."

"I think I see a pattern here, professor. Although Pat Farnsworth talks about her concern for the poor, she acts *against* their interests."

"Yes, that's exactly what I'm saying. Just as with education, she wants powerful backers with deep pockets. You've probably never heard of him, but a great economist named Thomas Sowell nailed the truth when he wrote a long time ago that 'ordinary people need a refuge from the rampaging presumptions of their betters'. Sadly, ordinary Americans have no refuge from politicians like Pat Farnsworth.

"Many politicians they talk about their lofty-sounding goals, but that's a cover for their lust for power. Pat Farnsworth craved the power to transform the U.S. and if some people had to be hurt in the process, too bad, but they were just collateral damage. As Walter Duranty put it, 'To make an omelet, you have to crack some eggs.'"

"Excuse me, professor. *Walter Duranty* said that? Who was he?"

"He was the *New York Times* correspondent in Moscow who was feted by Stalin and dutifully reported to the world that things were great in the Soviet Union, while in fact millions were being starved to death in the Ukraine. Appallingly, Duranty received a Pulitzer Prize for his writing. It's arguably the worst instance in history of the press covering up for terrible crimes by a ruler. A few years back, a movie was made about that."

"I will have to find that movie," said Jen, as she jotted down 'movie about Walter Duranty.'

Jen heard Oistrakh take a long breath.

"Are you getting tired, professor? We could resume our talk at another time if you'd like."

"No, no, Ms. Van Arsdale. Actually, I find this very stimulating. Around here, almost no one will listen when I criticize our former president, or attack her statist agenda. Instead, at Stanford, if you say something even the least bit negative about Farnsworth and her policies, you're apt to get your head bitten off—called a racist or fascist or something. I'm glad to have a chance to speak to someone who listens."

Jen knew that the same was true at the *Post* and throughout the media. Fear of being denounced as a traitor to leftist values kept many people from speaking their minds. That was why she felt the need to sneak into a concert that could be condemned as exemplifying "white privilege."

Jen also recognized that she never bothered listening to arguments against progressivism. She had been taught to automatically impugn the motives of anyone who said that free societies worked better than controlled ones, or that government policies usually had harmful unintended consequences. And here she was, listening to an elderly law professor who kept making such arguments.

All of those deep thinkers she had always admired—the ones who demonized people like Professor Oistrakh for questioning their vision—had been wrong. Jen regretted that her mind had for so many years been closed.

"I have to admit, professor, that I seldom speak with people of a conservative bent and I'm learning a lot."

Oistrakh laughed.

"I'm happy to hear you say that, but I don't regard myself as a conservative."

"You don't?"

"No, I regard myself as a liberal—a liberal in the true sense of the word. Liberalism arose in the seventeenth century when a few thinkers began to understand that people would be happier and more productive if they were freed from the constraints of the powerful institutions that dominated their lives—the interests of monarchs and church leaders and guilds.

"Liberals wanted to liberate people from those constraints—hence the term. They favored legal equality of all human beings—equality of opportunity without governmental favors or obstacles. They favored freedom to produce, to trade, to speak your mind, to worship or not, according to your own beliefs. They thought that government should keep order and protect the rights of the people, but otherwise to leave them alone. If you believe that people should have the liberty to run their lives, 'liberal' is the word for you.

"Liberalism is the one philosophy that requires no enemies—not foreigners, not people who have too much money, not people who believe in a different religion. It minimizes conflict and calls upon people to resolve whatever problems arise through peaceful means.

"Would you like to know where liberalism arose? I gather from your name that you have some Dutch ancestry. Well, it was the Dutch who first rejected the old, *conservative* notion that the only exalted sort of life was to be a noble, a clergyman, or a soldier. Common workers and traders had traditionally been looked down upon as inferiors. Humanity suffered from poverty, intolerance, and wars for thousands of years due to the control imposed by authoritarian elites.

"But for some reason, the Dutch started to reject that traditional view of society in the sixteenth century. They entertained the idea that it was perfectly fine to trade and make profits. That new, liberal way of looking at life resulted in a rising standing of living in the Netherlands. It freed up human energy and ingenuity to pursue commercial gains, rather than confining them to furthering the interests of the rulers. Liberalism spread to England, then slowly, often incompletely, to other parts of Europe. The scholar you should consult if you really want to understand this is Professor Deirdre McCloskey."

"Thanks, I will, professor," Jen replied as she jotted down another note.

"You'll find her books to be eye-opening, I believe. Now, as for the term 'conservative,' there certainly are many aspects of America worth conserving, but also many that we ought to jettison. The word 'liberal' is a more accurate description of my philosophy and I think it's time that it was rescued from the abuse it has taken for more than a century. Unfortunately, Americans started to think that 'liberal' meant policies of ever-expanding government control when in truth those policies were the *exact opposite* of liberal. They restored state power and diminished the sphere of liberty."

"I had never thought of things that way. Please tell me more about your philosophy, professor."

"Gladly. Liberalism is the philosophy of peace and cooperation. All others condone coercion and violence by some people against others. And since there are innumerable ideas about who should be allowed to coerce whom and for what reasons, you have unending conflict. Under liberalism, the only way for a person to improve his life is through cooperation with others. There is no place for the theft, exploitation, and domination that other systems invite. The government's role is at most to protect life, liberty, and property—never to become a menace to those rights as it so often does.

"Marxism justifies the expropriation of business and landowners who have, its advocates claim, exploited the workers. National socialism—Nazism—justifies extensive government controls over any aspect of life that affects the strength of the nation. That philosophy, by the way, still exists even though Hitler and his Thousand Year Reich were defeated. The world has lots of countries that differ little from Nazi Germany, except that they don't persecute Jews.

"Mercantilism calls for a host of economic mandates and prohibitions that supposedly lead to national economic power, but in fact keep most people poor. Progressivism demands an endless string of taxes and regulations and punishments in the name of that amorphous phrase 'social justice.' But progressivism actually impedes progress by putting government officials, who get paid whether they're right or wrong, over society's producers, who make money when they're right but lose it when they're wrong.

"Under those coercive, *illiberal* philosophies, the lives, liberties and property of ordinary people become expendable for some greater good—as envisioned by the powerful. They're the 'eggs' in the omelet."

Oistrakh paused, giving Jen the opportunity to ask, "Just a moment ago, professor, you said that social justice is just an amorphous phrase—I think that's how you put it. President Farnsworth used it constantly. Would you please explain what you mean?"

"Certainly. It's an amorphous phrase because society is not a thing and cannot act justly or unjustly or at all. It's just an abstraction. Only the actions of *people* can be called just or unjust. Their unjust actions should be criticized or rectified. But the term 'social justice' is meaningless because *society* doesn't act.

"When people use that phrase, they're complaining that they don't like the results of free interactions among people, such as the fact that black people have lower average incomes than white people do or that there are more men than women on science faculties. Social justice is the catch-phrase authoritarians use whenever they want more power. They know it usually disarms criticism when they say, 'This new law or program will advance social justice.'"

Jen had written about social justice thousands of times, and this professor just said that she was using an empty catch-phrase. That was something to ponder, but later.

"That certainly is an interesting point of view, professor. But under your philosophy of liberalism, don't the rich keep getting richer and the poor poorer? Don't we need to have government step in and redistribute wealth in the interests of equality and social stability?"

"Ah--that's a very good question! "

"I would guess that a sizeable majority of Americans believe that's true. The authoritarians have done a good job of misleading them. But it's not true that a liberal society is one in which the rich get richer, and the poor get poorer unless the government intervenes.

"First of all, the rich do get richer, but so does everyone else. Liberal societies enjoy a steady increase in the range of goods and services available in the market. They get better and better in quality and cost less and less to buy. To produce all those things, those 'rich' business owners—many of whom start out poor and become wealthier as they succeed—need to hire workers. They need to pay those workers enough to keep them from taking better offers from other businesses. In a liberal economy, everyone gains from the vast expansion of earning opportunities. It's not the case that, as we so often hear, wealth 'trickles down' from the rich to the poor, but rather that, due to the investments and innovations of rich people, the poor can earn far more than they could under the old order with its pervasive, top-down control.

"Secondly, the wealth accumulated by the rich gives them the ability to devote it to social problems. Unlike the wealthy nobles, rich business people donated huge sums to libraries, universities, and schools. Andrew Carnegie used his steel fortune to open public libraries. Julius Rosenwald devoted much of his Sears & Roebuck fortune to private schools for black children in the segregated South. Many others established charitable foundations, although they didn't always like the results. Henry Ford, for example, bitterly lamented that he couldn't defund the Ford Foundation.

"Under liberalism, some people get spectacularly rich because they produce what millions want to buy. Then, people who want them to use their money for good purposes can try to *convince* them to do so. That works out infinitely better than having the government *take* their money from them to be used as politicians want. Now, politicians are good at professing their commitment to solving problems and advancing the general welfare, but the truth is that they mostly spend tax money in ways that will help keep them in power. Instead of solving problems like poverty, they create programs that *perpetuate* them.

"People who worry that liberalism allows some to get extremely rich should stop and think that rich people do things with their money that mostly benefit the non-rich: they spend their money on goods and services provided by non-rich people; they invest their money in ways that create new job opportunities and new products for non-rich people; and they donate their money to charitable causes that aim at making life better for non-rich people. The more the government takes away from them, the less good they can do."

"All right, professor, that's a good argument, but if the rich get too rich, won't they be able to control our political system and use it for their own benefit?"

"That's another of Pat Farnsworth's justifications for heavy 'progressive' taxes. But it's a poor argument. You have to keep in mind that rich people often disagree with each other, so whatever political influence they have is pulling in different directions. The claim that the rich will take over our democracy is a fairy tale. But if you truly worry about it, the solution is to limit the scope of government authority so it can't do favors for anyone. That's what the Founders had in mind when they wrote the Constitution, giving the federal government very few powers.

"One more point. Once the plundering of the successful by democratic politics starts, it never stops. Government keeps engorging itself on the confiscated wealth. Interest groups demand more from the state and most politicians are happy to give it to them—in return for their support, of course. And as government grows, more and more people get in the habit of thinking that it can solve every problem by passing new laws or just handing out money. Hardly anyone considers the costs of the mega-state: its diversion of resources from productive uses, its encroachments on freedom, its spreading of falsehoods to sustain itself, and so on."

Stan Zygalski had said the same thing at the Free People meeting. It was an idea to ponder. But now, Jen decided it was time to get back to the reason for the call—to get more information about Pat Farnsworth and her political career.

"You make a very persuasive case for liberalism professor. Now, is there anything else you'd like to say about Pat Farnsworth's years as governor?"

Oistrakh drew a long breath.

"Yes, a lot, but let me sum things up this way. During her eight years, California retrogressed badly. Unemployment up. Poverty up. Business closures up, business starts down. Education got worse than ever. In many parts of the state, respect for the law has disappeared, and spreading crime terrifies peaceful people. And when those people would try to defend themselves against the criminals, she was all for prosecuting them for illegal gun use. And, apropos of your previous question, the rich did get richer and the poor got poorer. That's always the result of statism, the opposite of liberalism.

"California had been rotting under Democratic rule for many years, but under Pat Farnsworth, it was like watching the last years of the Roman Empire – speeded up."

"All right. How about her presidency?"

"Farnsworth's eight years in the White House did incalculable and irreparable harm to the nation. Her worst damage, I would say, was to the rule of law. Many presidents before her had harmed it, but theirs were just razor nicks compared to the way Farnsworth slit its throat."

Jen swallowed hard at that phrase. "Go on, please."

"First of all, Farnsworth subverted the rule of law by her innumerable executive orders. Under our Constitution, legislation is the business of Congress but the president now routinely makes new laws by issuing executive orders. Too bad that wasn't stopped in its tracks when FDR began using them to do things he wanted to do immediately rather than 'waiting' for Congress. This country isn't supposed to have an executive with dictatorial power, but presidents have grown bolder and bolder in using them. Pat Farnsworth far exceeded all of her predecessors. As a result, the separation of powers is a dead letter. The president can act as a dictator, and she often did.

"Next, think about her signature achievement of packing the Supreme Court with people who share her philosophy of unchecked central government power. On crucial issues of constitutional and statutory interpretation, we now have a court with no independence stuffed with judges chosen not for their legal acumen but because of their fidelity to leftist ideology.

"Those new justices she picked never engage in true legal analysis. They decide cases the way that their feelings or sympathies tell them to. Our traditional concepts of due process have been tossed aside by jurists who are fixated on which side should win to promote 'social justice.'

"Courts traditionally decided cases based on the written law, not on their feelings. Whether the parties before them have acted legally or not should have nothing to do with how rich or poor they are, whether they're in a 'marginalized group' or not.

"And when deciding whether a law is valid or not, the focus should be on its consonance with the written Constitution, not on the professed intentions of the politicians who passed it. But the justices now either ignore the Constitution or twist its words so they can decide the way they want to.

"What we are losing is the concept of neutral principles of law. That was one of the great things about America that brought millions of immigrants here in the 19th and 20th centuries.

"My own family came from Russia, where Jews often were treated as inferior citizens. In America, the law was the same for everybody. Your religion had nothing to do with it. People knew they could depend on courts to enforce contracts and settle disputes based on the law.

"That was one of the big reasons why people immigrated here by the millions. They knew that life here was hard, but legal equality meant that they could succeed based on their efforts, not on their origins. In America, the law was fixed and knowable. People could depend on it.

"Unfortunately, our Supreme Court has become a policy instrument, there to rubber-stamp anything Pat Farnsworth and her allies want. Justice is no longer blind but, instead, looks the parties over and figures out which side's victory would do more to cement their power.

"While I'm talking about the courts and the rule of law, I have to say something about the deplorable way Farnsworth used impeachment to remove lower court judges who decided cases 'the wrong way.' Very rarely had judges been impeached throughout our history and only for flagrantly illegal behavior such as taking bribes.

"But someone in her inner circle got the brilliant idea that impeachment could be used for political leverage, and with zealous Democrats in complete control, they said, 'Why not do it?'

"They came up with ancient, unverifiable complaints of misbehavior against a couple of federal district judges and one on the Sixth Circuit. The media breathlessly reported that the impeachments were about upholding 'judicial integrity' but in truth, they were about destroying it with dirty tricks.

"The Democrats got to fill empty seats with judges who were on their side, and the message went out to all judges not to anger them if they didn't want to be next. Since then, there has been a sharp increase in the number of times when judges recuse themselves from cases. It's because they don't want to choose between rendering a decision they know is wrong and facing an impeachment circus.

"As a result of Pat Farnsworth's machinations, we no longer have an independent judiciary. We have one that obeys the regime in Washington."

Oistrakh coughed but immediately continued.

"We also see the erosion of the rule of law in the way defendants are treated. You may remember that some years ago, a conservative writer named Dinesh D'Souza was actually sent to prison over a tiny infraction of a vague campaign finance statute, but under Farnsworth's administration, government agents who were found to have lied in court documents were let off with barely a slap on the wrist. Both send a message—the justice system is no longer blind, but cares which side you're on. A politicized justice system is no longer truly a justice system, but just another aspect of the rulers' never-ending campaign to retain power."

Jen knew about the impeachments and had justified them in one of her columns—without doing anything to check the veracity of the allegations. At the time, that seemed the right thing to do—get rid of stodgy conservative judges in favor of new ones attuned to the times. The downside of losing judicial independence hadn't occurred to her. She was troubled by the professor's point that punishment could depend on your political allegiance.

"Professor, I see your point about the importance of an independent judiciary and retaining the neutral rule of law. But now I would like to ask you about something else if I might. A minute ago you referred to your family coming here from Russia. Your name is uncommon. You wouldn't perhaps be related to..."

"To David Oistrakh? Why yes, I suspect that they are related. My great grandfather left Russia for the United States late in the nineteenth century and other Oistrakhs stayed. David Oistrakh was born in Odessa in 1908 and became one of the most famous violinists of the twentieth century. I own many of his recordings and tried writing to him when I was a young man hoping to confirm a family lineage. Unfortunately, I don't think my letter got through to him since the Cold War was still going on. Since you mention him, I take it that you're knowledgeable about classical music."

Another music lover! Jen pounced.

"Yes, it's one of the great loves of my life. I think that David Oistrakh's recording of the Tchaikovsky Concerto with Eugene Ormandy and the Philadelphia Orchestra is unbeatable. And his performances of Shostakovich's A minor concerto were legendary."

"It's very nice to hear you say that, Ms. Van Arsdale. Shostakovich wrote the concerto for David in the late 1940s, but it wasn't premiered until 1955, after Stalin was safely dead. Do you know that Shostakovich lived in dread of Stalin's regime?"

"No, I've never heard that. I'd like to know more."

"He absolutely did. Anyone who displeased Stalin in any way was apt to be arrested, put on trial before judges he had approved, convicted without any fuss over procedure and evidence, then either sent to the Gulag or summarily executed.

"By 1936, Shostakovich had written an opera entitled *Lady Macbeth of the Mtsensk District*. When it was premiered in Moscow, Stalin himself was present and walked out with his entourage before the end of the opera. When Shostakovich was informed of that, he went white, fearing it meant disapproval from The Great Leader. The next day, *Pravda* ran a very hostile review of the work, which was assumed to come from Stalin himself.

"Shostakovich was then attacked in print by many Soviet musical figures, and those few who defended him were arrested. For years, he lived in terror.

"Eventually, he was able to regain favor with the regime through some excellent pieces that it approved—such as his Fifth Symphony—and some groveling ones written simply to flatter Stalin. But in 1948 he was again denounced and another anti-Shostakovich campaign was launched. The Violin Concerto, with its brooding tone that seems to be his lament for Stalin's victims, had to be kept under wraps until the cultural thaw after Stalin's death."

"That's frightening history".

"To say the least. Now let me ask you another question. Have you ever heard of Lavrenti Beria?"

"No, I don't think I have."

"Beria was Stalin's head of security, an utterly ruthless man who cared nothing for human life. It was he who oversaw Stalin's order to execute over fourteen thousand captured Polish officers in 1941.

"Beria is said to have remarked to Stalin, 'Give me the man, and I will find you the crime.' Under the vague Soviet laws, you see, he could plausibly accuse almost anyone of some crime. Solzhenitsyn's *Gulag Archipelago* provides many horrifying examples. And with a completely obedient judiciary, there was no fairness, no due process of law. You had one-party rule and a terrified populace.

"The reason I mention that is because the U.S. has been sliding in that same direction—many vague laws and innumerable regulations that give the government discretion to assail almost anyone. Federal bureaucrats can bring action against people for violations of regulations they had no reason to believe existed."

"I have heard about that," said Jen, thinking back to Lisa Burdette's encounters with the social responsibility officials.

"This has been a growing problem for decades, but at least in the old days, there were independent judges who would slap down the politicians and bureaucrats when they went too far in interpreting their mandates or failed to treat the accused to due process of law.

"But now, thanks to President Farnsworth, we have far more laws and regulations than ever, covering even formerly sacred domains like freedom of speech, and a judiciary that is full of true believers who care very little about due process. We don't have a Gulag and don't execute people who displease the regime, but the effect is the same. Americans are being cowed by a ruling party that can and will use the law to go after those who get out of line.

"It's impossible to overstate the seriousness of this development. We are *retrogressing* in terms of human society. There was a great English legal philosopher in the nineteenth century, Sir Henry Sumner Maine, who wrote that the history of human progress was the history of our advancement from a society based on *status* to one based on *contract*. In the former, people have privileges assigned based on their social group. In the latter, individuals deal with each other voluntarily, as equals.

"It was precisely that contract society that made it possible for people from unpopular groups, such as the Jews and the Chinese, to succeed in America. Many Americans disliked those groups, but the law protected their property and their freedom to deal as equals with anyone who wanted to give them a chance. That environment made it possible for anyone to succeed, and most did.

"But there's a problem—societies based on contract lead to inequalities that envious people can't tolerate. Then politicians like Pat Farnsworth step in to capitalize on that envy by promising to even everything out. That means ditching legal equality and freedom of contract. We are much worse off for returning to an ancient mode of social organization. Like a malignant tumor, its harm is spreading."

"And none of that would happen under your liberal philosophy, right, professor?"

"That is correct."

"Professor, could we now turn specifically to the First Amendment? I take it that you disapprove of the Anti-Hate Speech Law."

"Oh, I certainly do. Under the First Amendment, such a law is—or I guess I should say, *was*—blatantly unconstitutional. The men who wrote the Constitution knew that if the government had the power to interfere with speech, that power would surely be used to stifle criticism of the government and punish those who advanced unpopular ideas. That's why they wrote an absolute ban on laws that abridged the freedom of speech or press into the Constitution. They understood that the realm of thought had to be kept free of coercion.

"Then we get Pat Farnsworth and her cadre of loyal, authoritarian Democrats. First, they stack the Supreme Court with ideological allies; then they enact a law that mocks the spirit of the First Amendment, but which is ruled constitutional—as the 'People's Court' now interprets it. 'Hate speech' has no protection, and 'hate speech' means whatever the members of the Anti-Hate Speech Commission—all cronies of Farnsworth—say it means.

"They claim that they aren't involved in censorship. Americans are supposedly still free to speak and write, provided that they don't say anything that's 'hateful'. That freedom, however, is illusory.

"Activists who want to harass or silence voices they don't like can file charges with the Commission, which the defendant must answer. Going through that administrative process by itself is punishing. In the end, most defendants are fined. But this, of course, is a one-way street. Complaints by conservatives or libertarians or religious people about *hate speech against them* are automatically dismissed. As out-group members, they don't deserve the new privilege of free speech.

"Justice Holmes foresaw this more than a century ago. In a famous dissent, he wrote, 'Persecution for the expression of opinions seems to me perfectly logical. If you have no doubt of your premises of your power and want a certain result with all your heart, you naturally express your wishes in law and sweep away all opposition.' His words describe the people now fully in control of our government.

"The First Amendment is dying under a purportedly well-meaning law to protect people from 'harmful' words and to make them feel safe. But what's actually going on is that the ruling elite is using the law to silence criticism so it can keep its grip on power.

"Beria had his vague law—he could call anything 'anti-Soviet activity'—and now we have 'hate speech' which is used in exactly the same manner. Its object is a 'despotism over the mind' as a fellow retired professor dared to say before he was hauled before the Commission and fined.

"The horrifying truth is that here in the U.S., we now have a powerful cadre of politicians, academics, and tech leaders who are just as hostile to freedom of speech as the Soviets were. In my long career in the law, I never thought I'd see a concerted attack on the First Amendment, but it's gaining strength.

"Pat Farnsworth has no more attachment to free speech than did Stalin or Brezhnev. Her successor is no better and her minions are determined to the remaining islands of free speech and press. Those of us who argue against this trend are vilified, harassed, shouted down, hounded out of jobs and so on by government officials, business leaders, faculty zealots, and student mobs. This is going to end badly for America."

Jen thought a moment, then said, "All right, professor. I see your concern. But isn't there *something* to be said for a law that cracks down on hate speech? Some people really do use speech in a hateful way that demeans others and could lead to violence."

Oistrakh cleared his throat.

"No, I don't think there is anything to be said for it. Almost everything that Farnsworth and her allies label as 'hate speech' is just speech that they disagree with. In America, our tradition was that if someone said something you disliked, found offensive, or thought completely wrong, you used your own freedom of speech to argue back. Or you simply ignored it. What you didn't do was run to the government to whine about it because the government had no authority to do anything. But now it does have authority and that is having a terrible effect. Debate and the flow of information are being curtailed on the silly and transparently political pretext that words are equivalent to violence.

"I'm sure you've heard Lord Acton's saying that 'Power corrupts and absolute power corrupts absolutely.' Well, what power could be more corrupting than the power to control what people may say? The end game here for Pat Farnsworth and millions of her fellow authoritarians is to control how people think. No government should have that power.

"Let me make one more point, and then I think we should call a halt for today, Ms. Van Arsdale.

"The way the Commission works is to target conservative, libertarian, and classical liberal voices that 'progressives' want silenced. Mark my words, though—in time, that same power will be used against honest critics on the left who think that the government's policies have become harmful or that officials are acting to further their own interests. What goes around comes around, as the saying goes.

"And that brings me back to Beria. After Stalin died, he wanted to take over, but other Soviets leaders had him arrested and shot. *What goes around comes around.*"

"I agree that this is a good stopping point, professor. This has been a most interesting conversation, Professor Oistrakh.

I must say that I have learned a lot from it—about the former president and other things. I hope that I might call back another day if I have more questions for you."

"I have also enjoyed our conversation, and you certainly may call back any time. I have much more to say on the damage Pat Farnsworth has inflicted on America—but now I need to rest."

Jen leaned back on her sofa to think about the two conversations she'd had.

Two people who knew the real Pat Farnsworth had given her thumbs down on personal character and public policies. Professor Swensen thought she had wrecked higher education. Professor Oistrakh thought she had destroyed the rule of law.

Was Pat Farnsworth's vision for America leading not to a bright future but to one of ruthless control by a governing elite?

Writing a book proclaiming Pat Farnsworth as a great president was looking hard, if not impossible.

Jen went to her computer and googled "movie about Walter Duranty."

CHAPTER 10

Trouble in Alexandria

After her conversation with Alexander Oistrakh, Jen set up her taxi ride to Maddy's house for Bonnie's birthday party. Then she jotted down key points from her conversations with Nicole Swensen and Alex Oistrakh.

According to both, Pat Farnsworth had done irreparable damage to the country. She hadn't led America into her 'radiant future,' but instead had done much to demolish its foundations. If they were right, the future wasn't radiant but dismal.

Ever since her Oberlin days, Jen had been certain that America needed massive social and economic reforms of just the kind that President Farnsworth had achieved. Wages had been raised, education brought under unified control, ancient inequities corrected, jobs and health care guaranteed for everyone, taxes imposed more justly, speech regulated so that it had to be responsible, and much, much more.

It all fit together into a beautiful whole—the great social and economic reforms that Jen had extolled for years in her writing had been achieved. America was finally under the control of people with the right ideals.

And yet, she was hearing from obviously sensible people that the country was in deep trouble. Soaring prices. Rising crime and unemployment. Businesses closing. Schools failing to educate. People treated unfairly by abusive officials.

Things ought to be getting better under progressive control, but they were instead getting *worse*. The meeting with the Free People of Laguna Beach had convinced Jen of that.

Apparently, there *was* something to the argument of right-wing economists that she had so often dismissed—that government actions usually had bad unintended consequences. Maybe the people who made those arguments didn't make them out of evil motives, as she'd always assumed, but because they understood that government policies would damage the very people they were supposed to help.

What if they were right? What if there was an underlying order to society that government interventions, even if well-intentioned, caused to go awry?

And what if those government interventions were not well-intentioned, but were done to make life better for those who had their hands on power? If businessmen were greedy and self-interested, why believe that government officials were any better?

It was almost heretical to think that government might be the cause of problems rather than the solution. *Ronald Reagan had said that*. But Jen had to admit that there was much to be said for it.

Jen thought about Maddy, who had for many years politely raised those objections when the subject of politics came up. Perhaps she wasn't just a silly little kid after all. She hadn't gone to college but had nevertheless learned a lot just from her reading. Her library *was* impressive. Jen had always brushed off her sister's failure to embrace progressivism as the unfortunate result of right-wing radio she sometimes listened to and the business interests of her in-laws—that her mind had been contaminated and couldn't function properly.

When Maddy would say something like 'The state is our enemy and the bigger it grows, the more harm it does,' she just rolled her eyes. Once she had even rebuked her, saying, 'Maddy, you didn't even go to college, so who are you to question experts who did?' At the time, Jen was sorry for that unkind jab. Now she was doubly sorry for it.

Each time she had visited Maddy's home, Jen walked past her shelves of books, avoiding them as if they gave off poisonous gases. Why did she waste her time and money on them, she always wondered? *But they might be worth reading.*

Did Maddy own that book Nicole Swenson had mentioned, *The Road to Serfdom*? This evening she would ask about it.

Jen understood that she needed to widen her scope of inquiry. She had been wearing blinders since college. They had to come off.

Throughout her career in journalism, Jen had always pitched her columns to show that any problem in America was due to Republicans, business interests, constitutional zealots, or other backward-thinking people. No problem was ever caused by Democrats, left-wing interest groups, unions, or government policies. Conversely, solutions worth considering always entailed new laws or more regulation, never repealing existing laws.

She thought of the question from that Navajo woman in the Phoenix debate. Pat Farnsworth had thought it would put her in mortal peril if that 'what laws would you repeal?' question started to get traction. But why keep it suppressed? Maybe it would be a good thing if Americans started asking candidates which laws they would repeal, and not settling for empty slogans and evasions.

Jen looked at the world the way she did because it was *expected*. She would never have gotten where she was, with the *Washington Post* and books in her name published by reputable firms if she had ever deviated from the progressive script. Independent thought was a ticket to oblivion, as much in the U.S. as it had been in Shostakovich's Soviet Union.

She had seen younger writers chastised for even thinking of writing pieces that didn't reinforce the belief in the wisdom and benevolence of the state. On a few occasions, older writers or editors had been dismissed. Jen hadn't been troubled by any of that because she believed it was *harmful* to cause people to doubt the good intentions of government officials and the efficacy of their programs.

But maybe that wasn't the case. What if the people who said they wanted to reform the country were only looking out for themselves? And what if the people who said they could fix our society were just as arrogant and foolish as the people who said they could fix classical music by supplanting merit with diversity?

Jen had dropped off to sleep on her sofa when the phone rang. She reached for it and saw that it was Maddy.

"Oh, hi, Maddy. What's up?"

"Jen, there's a riot in Alexandria! Do you have the TV on?"

Jen clicked the TV on, and the screen showed a mob on King Street, throwing bottles and bricks at heavily outnumbered police, smashing store windows, and running off with merchandise. Many in the mob had signs reading, 'Justice for Jeri!' Other signs read, 'It's Not Looting, It's Social Justice.'

"This is terrible, Maddy!"

"Jen, I can't reach Josh, He was in the store and was going to close up and leave at five. I've called again and again and he doesn't answer. I'm afraid he might be hurt."

"I'll come over right now."

"No, don't! "The main streets are blocked off, and you shouldn't walk in the area. Stay there, and I'll call you as soon as I hear something."

Breathing heavily, Jen returned to the action on her TV screen.

The reporter, Theresa Tommassini, was pointing to a mob about one hundred yards down the street from her, saying, "The protest broke out earlier this afternoon, shortly after sixteen-year-old Jerilyn Barton was found gagged and tied inside a dumpster just a block from King Street. Police were alerted to muffled sounds coming from the dumpster by a passer-by. At the scene, the police found Ms. Barton inside the dumpster, which had been spray-painted, 'Go Back Where You Came From.'

"In her statement, Ms. Barton told the police that she had been walking on King Street that afternoon when she was abducted by three young white men with very short hair and tattoos, who gagged her, tied her up, and put her into the dumpster.

"Within an hour after Ms. Barton gave her statement, a mob of protesters appeared on King Street, rapidly swelling in numbers to the several hundred you can see behind me. The protesters shouted, 'No Justice, No Peace' as they began to smash windows and take goods from shops."

As Theresa Tommassini continued speaking, the camera zoomed in on the scene, and Jen could see the sign above one of the looted shops: White's Music.

Jen's phone rang again—it was Maddy.

"Oh, Jen. I still can't get Josh. I think he's in the store, injured. I got as close as I could and told an officer that my husband was inside White's Music, probably hurt. They've called for reinforcements so they can control the mob and get into the most damaged area."

On her TV, Jen could see about thirty officers in riot gear start moving down King Street. The rioters threw things at the police phalanx, then ran in all different directions, many carrying looted goods.

One item caught Jen's eye—a trumpet.

As Jen continued to watch, she saw two officers enter White's Music. A minute later, an ambulance rolled down King Street and stopped in front of the store. Paramedics went in with a stretcher and soon reemerged with a body on it. They loaded the stretcher into the ambulance, which sped away with its lights flashing and siren blaring.

Maddy called again.

"Jen, Josh *was* in the store. He was beaten and is unconscious. They're taking him to Inova Hospital. I'll call you when I know how he is."

Jen couldn't bear to watch the TV any longer. She turned it off and then put her head in her hands and sobbed.

For almost an hour, Jen remained immobilized on her sofa. When her phone rang, she grabbed it, expecting news from Maddy. Instead, the call was from her editor, Gabrielle Tartakover.

"Hi, Jen," she said. "We want to put out a story on the Alexandria protests for tomorrow. Think you could dash something off?"

Jen had never said 'no' to an editor before, but today was different.

"Gabrielle, I'm sorry but I can't. I'm awfully tired and we really don't know very much about the protest at this point. And we shouldn't leap to hasty conclusions, as we did in the Nick Sandmann case."

"But Jen, you've written lots of pieces on protests. You know—the deep and painful grievances causing spontaneous protests from people in the community, yada, yada, yada."

She certainly had written that kind of piece before. Not today.

"No, Gabrielle. You'll have to get someone else."

Jen tossed her phone down on the sofa. Five minutes later, it rang again. This time it was Maddy.

"Maddy, what's the news about Josh?"

"He'll be all right, Jen. The doctor said he had a serious concussion and suffered three broken ribs from being kicked. Maybe some kidney damage, too. He has regained consciousness, and I spoke with him a few minutes ago.

"He said that when the rioters broke into the store, he told them that they could take the money in the register and anything they wanted. But when they started smashing stringed instruments, he tried to stop them. They knocked him down and started kicking and beating him, saying, 'Take this, Mister White Music.' He blacked out and the next thing he knew, he was on a stretcher looking up at a paramedic."

"Oh, what a relief to hear that, Maddy. What room is he in? I'd like to visit this evening."

"He's in Room 449. I hear that riots have broken out elsewhere in Alexandria, but the hospital area should be safe."

"I'll be there in an hour."

Jen was in the taxi on the way to Inova Hospital when her phone rang. It was Will Collier.

"Hi, Will. How are you?"

"I'm fine, Jen, but I heard about the rioting in your area. It's not close to you, is it?"

"Thanks for asking, Will. No, the riots are several miles away from where I live, but my brother-in-law was attacked by some of the rioters when they broke into his music store. He was beaten unconscious and has some broken ribs, but he'll be okay. I'm on my way to see him right now."

"Damn," said Will. "All that violence over a hoax."

"You think it was *a hoax*, Will?"

"I'd bet my Oldsmobile on it. The dumpster story is extremely fishy. Three skinhead punks abduct this hefty girl in broad daylight and spray paint the dumpster. And right after this 'crime' is discovered, a host of protesters show up, with signs, rocks, bottles and shopping bags. If the police decide to investigate this, I'm certain they will find that the whole thing was planned."

"*Planned*, Will? You think that some people *wanted* a riot here?"

"Yes, that's exactly it, Jen. Riots get people's attention. Riots keep the victimization idea boiling. Riots get people stuff."

"Thanks so much for calling, Will. I'm just getting to the hospital. We'll talk again soon."

When Jen entered Room 449, Maddy was sitting in a chair pulled close to the bed. She was holding Josh's hand. His head was bandaged and an IV was dripping a fluid into his arm.

"Hi, Josh. I'm so glad you're okay. You look pretty banged up. How long will you need to stay in the hospital?"

"Thanks for coming, Jen. The doc says I should be out in a day or two."

"At least your hands weren't damaged. You'll be able to get back to playing Bach's Cello Suites before long."

Josh smiled and moved his hands as if playing.

"Do you want to tell me what happened?" Jen asked.

"I heard a lot of unusual noise outside and knew trouble was coming. I told the sales clerk, Loretta, to leave by the back door. I locked the front door and crouched down behind the counter. Within a minute or two, I heard glass breaking and rioters broke in.

"Three men in masks saw me and told me to get up. I did, and told them to take the small amount of cash in the register. A few more rioters came in and started grabbing instruments they could carry like trumpets and clarinets. Then one of them started smashing the violins and violas on display with a pipe. I know I should have kept still, but I couldn't help myself. I ran to try to stop him. That's when two of them knocked me down and began kicking and punching me. Then I felt a blow to my head and everything went black."

"You always loved the strings most, Josh," said Maddy. "But it could have cost you your life. Next time, don't be a hero."

"Okay, honey. I've learned my lesson."

The three talked for a while before Maddy said, "I should get going and pick up Bonnie at your parents' house, Josh. I'll be back in the morning."

Then she turned to Jen.

"How about if I save you the cost of a taxi and drop you at your house?"

"Good idea. I'd sure enjoy your company, Maddy."

On the way to her townhouse, Jen said, "I have some stuff to tell you, Maddy. Remember earlier today when I mentioned that I met some people with brains out in California? People who were all very critical of President Farnsworth and her progressive policies. They were all regular people in a town that's hurting from crime and unemployment and inflation and government corruption. "

"Sure, I remember that."

"Well, there's much more to that story.

"One evening after a day of interviewing Pat Farnsworth, I went into the nearly town of Laguna Beach. After dinner and the sunset, I was walking along Pacific Coast Highway. My hat blew off and I chased it down a side street, where I was grabbed by a couple of men and dragged into an alley. I'm sure they intended to rape me—maybe even kill me."

"Jen, why didn't you tell me before now?" Maddy asked in an agitated voice.

"I didn't tell you because you and Josh have enough on your minds. And I was fine—scared out of my mind, but fine. Now, the only reason why I'm fine is that a man came along and chased away the two men who attacked me. He wasn't a cop, but had a gun and obviously knew how to use it.

"Maddy, you're probably thinking 'I told you so' about guns saving lives when they're in the right hands. *And you'd be right*. The guy—Will Collier is his name—shouldn't have had that gun under the new federal law, but he did have it and if he hadn't, I might not be here today."

They were at a stoplight and Maddy looked over at her sister.

"Jen, I wasn't going to say 'I told you so,' but I will say that it's a good thing that some laws can't be enforced against people who stand up for their rights."

"You're so right about that."

"Anyway, on my way to the hospital, Will called me. He had heard about the riot in Alexandria and wanted to know if I was all right. I told him that I was, but that Josh had been beaten up pretty badly. Will then said that he thought this whole thing was a hoax to spur a planned riot. I would have never considered that possibility before, but I think he's right."

"So do I, Jen. They've gotten away with this kind of thing before."

"After Will saved me from the thugs, he drove me back to my hotel, and we talked for a long time over coffee. He mentioned a neighborhood group he's involved with and invited me to their meeting, which was scheduled for the following evening. Those people get together every week to talk about how they can help each other, interesting things they've read, historical stuff—whatever is on their minds.

"Guess what? They all pretty much thought the same way you do, Maddy. They believe that freedom works and government usually makes things worse. One man talked about the difference between Makers and Takers and how countries go into decline once the Takers get the upper hand. That's basically what you've been saying, isn't it?"

"Yes, that's *exactly* what I've been saying. People cooperate very well to produce what they need and to solve their problems, but if government has the power to help some and hurt others, it's a certainty that people will begin to manipulate it to get what they want."

"I get that now, Maddy. Those people also made the point that politicians often manipulate voters with slogans and symbols meant to keep them from seeing reality. For example, Pat Farnsworth's big National Unity campaign. I always thought that sounded good and never doubted that it was working to bring America together.

"But the people I talked to—Black, white, Asian, Hispanic—thought it was just a waste of money. They didn't care about statues and monuments and names on buildings. They didn't feel hurt by them before and their lives are no better now that they're gone."

"And what do you think, Jen?"

Jen took a long breath.

"I think I agree. Maybe politics is mainly about manipulating people to get power and privilege, not about righting wrongs and building a just society."

"Sounds as though you've gotten quite an education in the last week, sis."

"Yes, and much more education came earlier today. I spoke with two people who knew Pat Farnsworth when she was in college and in law school. Both of them said that she's bossy, arrogant, vindictive, and so full of herself that she's dangerous. Of course, she is charming in person, but that's a mask for her ruthless ambition to be in charge of everything.

"From one of them, her college roommate, I learned that 'people of color' are not some big voting bloc, but individuals who think for themselves and don't like being stereotyped as aggrieved victims. From the other, a law professor, I learned that the word 'liberal' has been distorted. It shouldn't be used to describe the programs of politicians like Pat Farnsworth. Their programs, he argues, are illiberal, even *authoritarian.*

"From my conversation with him, I have to say that you're actually a liberal."

Maddy laughed.

"You're right, Jen, but it would confuse people if I said that."

Jen cleared her throat.

"And while I'm unburdening myself, I have come to realize that my profession, journalism, is guilty of pushing the country along a ruinous path. We always spin everything as proving that we need more government activism. Any environmental problem proved that we had to have draconian policies administered by Democrats. Any racial incident proved that we had to change the educational curriculum and institute more diversity programs. Any intemperate harangue by a conservative proved that need to toss aside the First Amendment and create federal a censorship commission run by Democrats and enforced only against people they dislike. Any slowing of the economy proved that we needed a load of federal stimulus spending.

"In short, *everything* is pitched to make people believe that more government is the solution to any problem. Say anything in favor of voluntary action or critical of the government, and your career will vanish.

"Most of us journalists believe that we're doing the right thing, but I suspect that many also go along with the ideological program because it meant good money and job security. The last man I spoke with, the law professor – who, by the way, is related to David Oistrakh – told me about Walter Duranty, the *New York Times* writer who was paid well to cover up Stalin's mass murders – you've probably heard about that haven't you, Maddy?"

"Yes, I read about Stalin and Duranty years ago. It makes your blood run cold."

"It certainly does. Unfortunately, there are thousands of Duranty types doing journalism in America. Just as Duranty didn't want people to know the truth about Stalin, most of my colleagues don't want people to know the truth about Pat Farnsworth and all the politicians like her. They *knowingly* deceive readers and receive accolades for doing so.

"The country is like a sinking ship, but journalists are too busy living it up in the lounge to inform the passengers of that fact. They're comfortably numb and think everyone else should be too. "

"Well, all this new knowledge puts you in something of a bind, doesn't it, Jen? You're expected to write a glowing biography about our first woman president who supposedly did so incredibly much to improve America, but now you've found out that she's a lousy person who pushed harmful ideas. What are you going to do?"

"I just don't know, Maddy. *I just don't know*. But here's one thing I know. I have got to read some of your books. Do you have one entitled *The Road to Serfdom*?"

"I do, and you can borrow as many of my books as you want."

Back in her home, Jen turned on the TV.

CNN was still covering the riot—or rather, the "protests"—and the announcer said, "We have heard from many of our political leaders about today's incident in Alexandria, Virginia.

"Just within the last few minutes, former President Patricia Farnsworth put out this statement, 'While I deplore the property damage and personal injuries suffered in today's protest, we must understand the militancy of Americans who have suffered for so long. The protest was mostly peaceful, resulting in only some minor injuries and property damage. Never forget that our First Amendment absolutely protects the right of Americans to air their grievances.'"

At that moment, Jen made up her mind what to do.

CHAPTER 11

Launching the Book

Throughout the rest of May, June, July, August, September, and October, Jen worked feverishly, like Handel while he was writing *Messiah*. She wrote whenever ideas entered her brain—the time of day or night didn't matter.

On November 1, she emailed Courtney Oliver to tell him that the book was ready. She had titled it *Patricia Farnsworth—A Life in Service to America*. He wrote back, asking her to email the manuscript to him.

Two weeks later, he emailed her back, writing, "The President loves the book exactly as it is. She says that you wrote precisely the biography she was expecting. I will forward the manuscript to our publisher. They're going to put it on the fast track so we can get it out before Christmas. The next step will be the book's launch and publicity campaign. I'll speak with the publisher about that, but am inclined to think that we'd do best to get you on that popular women's show *Today with Felicity* to blast off the campaign. That will mean a great audience that will go wild for the book. Felicity's viewership is enormous."

Jen wrote back that the plans sounded good to her, especially the national TV.

Everything went smoothly, and December sixteen was set as the launch date, with Jen to appear on *Today with Felicity* that morning. She woke very early with a feeling of anxiety. She had been on TV a few times, but this was going to be completely different.

Jen had thought through what she'd say dozens of times. Would she sound all right? Would she stumble and make a fool of herself? How would the host, Felicity Mantilla, react? What about the audience? There were so many variables to worry about that it was best not to worry about any of them.

The first decision of the day was what to wear. Jen went to her closet and chose a dark blue dress and matching shoes, thinking that she wanted a dignified look for the show. She dressed, petted Allegro, drank a glass of orange juice, then left the house.

A taxi took Jen to the studio. The show aired at 9:00, but the TV people wanted her there an hour early. She walked in at 8:01.

A young staffer met Jen and took her to the makeup room, where the show's makeup expert fussed over her face and hair for what Jen thought was a ridiculous amount of time. After that, she was escorted to the "green room" to wait.

Jen checked her phone—still thirty-three minutes until air time.

She checked again—twenty-six minutes. Her pulse was way above normal.

At a quarter before the hour, Felicity Mantilla walked in.

"Hello. You must be Jennifer Van Arsdale," she said in a chirpy voice. "I'm Felicity. So glad to have you on my show this morning!"

Felicity was tall and stringy, with long, jet black hair. She wore a tan pantsuit with a bright orange blouse and scads of gold jewelry. The contrast between the two women was striking.

"I'm pleased to meet you, Felicity. Your show is fantastic."

Actually, Jen had never seen *Today with Felicity*, but it seemed like the right thing to say.

"Thanks, Jennifer. Or what do you like to be called? Jenny?"

"Please call me Jen."

"Okay, Jen. We will have a copy of your book on the table between us. I'll hold it up so viewers can get a good look at the cover. I'll ask you some questions about what it was like to interview President Farnsworth, to delve into her career, to pick the brains of people who knew her earlier in life, and so on. After I do my introduction, I'll ask you to join me on stage for a nice discussion about your book. Okay?"

"Okay, Felicity. I'm ready."

At exactly 9:00, the show's producer, Wes Abramowicz, cued Felicity, who did not exactly walk out on stage, but rather did sort of a twirling dance. When she came to a stop, she looked out at the audience and said loudly, "Are we ready for a great program this Monday morning?"

From the audience came an enthusiastic "Yes. We. Are."

"Great! I am sure we're going to have one. My guest today is Jennifer Van Arsdale, the author of a new book being released today, the biography of America's first woman president, Pat Farnsworth. Please come out and join me, Jen!"

The waiting was finally over.

Jen walked out on stage, shook hands with Felicity, then sat in the guest's chair, placed to Felicity's right. On the table between them was a copy of *Pat Farnsworth – A Life in Service to America*, with its beaming photo of Pat on the cover.

Facing the audience, Felicity said, "Our guest writes for the *Washington Post* and has been in journalism ever since her college days. Jen, please tell us something about yourself and how you came to write the biography of President Pat Farnsworth."

"First of all, I am so glad to be on your show, Felicity. I really hope I'll be able to connect with your studio audience and viewers around the world."

"Some of you," said Jen, looking out across the packed room, "probably know that I have long been a supporter of Pat Farnsworth and her national unity agenda. Back in May when I was selected to write her biography, I could hardly wait to get into it, interviewing our former president for several days in her magnificent California home, speaking with people who knew her early in her life, poring through her official papers—doing all the research necessary to get to really know the woman and her accomplishments."

Felicity was smiling and nodding at Jen while playing with her big, gold necklace.

"After interviewing President Farnsworth, I did a lot of research, then dove into writing the book, which took nearly six months. You see it here on the table. It has just gone on sale today as Felicity said."

Felicity picked up the book and held it up for all to see.

Looking straight into the camera, Jen said, "The book Felicity is holding is exactly the book I anticipated writing and which Pat Farnsworth expected. It's celebratory. It tells Pat's story."

Applause rippled through the audience. Jen took a deep breath. *Now.*

"But during my research for the book, a strange thing happened—I encountered some people who gave me an entirely different perspective on the former president. In fact, they and subsequent events convinced me that Pat Farnsworth was *not* a good president. In fact, I am now convinced that she has brought America to the brink of ruin."

Jen glanced at Felicity, who was staring at her with an open mouth.

Keep going and don't let anything distract you from saying what you want to say, Jen thought.

"Instead of building national unity, Pat Farnsworth has sought to impose conformity on America. Disagree with her and you will be harassed, taxed, and silenced by her bureaucratic minions. She calls that 'progressive,' but it's very regressive. She undermined our economy, sent prices soaring, and then blamed others for all the troubles she caused. Businesses are closing, ambitious people are leaving, and the country is fast decaying. As a friend in California said, we're like a once-magnificent building whose foundation has been wrecked."

Some people in the audience were starting to talk. Jen heard one woman shout, "What the hell's wrong with her?" Another yelled, "Get her out of here! She offends me!"

Offstage, Wes Abramowicz bit his lip and wondered what to do. Could he get in trouble for allowing this to continue? *How would this affect ratings?* There were still three minutes before the first commercial break. He decided to let the show continue.

Jen heard Felicity take a breath to say something, but she wanted to fend-off interruptions. She hurried on to get out as much of her carefully rehearsed statement as possible.

"I learned that many things I had believed all my adult life were wrong. I learned that government never creates prosperity, but does a lot to impede it. That our education system is now much more about controlling minds than about opening them. That the politicians who talk so much about their concern and compassion are using that rhetoric as a cover for their lust for power."

Felicity started to say, "What..." but Jen spoke more loudly as she continued.

"For all those reasons, I actually wrote *two* books—this one on the table and a second one that I regard as the antidote for it. That book, which I have entitled *Pat Farnsworth—Serving Herself at Our Expense* is available for free online. You can download it at Free People LB dot net. That's Free People LB dot net. In that book, I try to explain why our vast, incredibly costly, and authoritarian government is the enemy of peace and prosperity. I hope that Americans will read both of my books and make up their minds."

Felicity couldn't remain quiet any longer. She reached out and touched the biography.

"Are you saying that you *disown* this book? Are you really telling us that you don't think Pat Farnsworth was a great president?"

Jen looked straight at her and replied, "Actually, Felicity, I came to the conclusion that she was our *worst* president. We've had bad presidents before, but Pat Farnsworth has driven America past the point of no return. She has ruined our economy and done irreparable damage to the rule of law. Thanks to her, we've become a nation with far more Takers than Makers.

"Pat Farnsworth didn't get her way because of her intellect or persuasion. She got her way through brute force, then cemented her power by destroying political dialogue and turning our elections into farces. And she relied on journalists like me to help condition people to accept that we need an omnipotent government."

Jen turned to look into the camera.

"You may not want to hear this, but Pat Farnsworth and her statist allies have torpedoed the American way of life and our ship is sinking fast."

From the audience came more shouts. "Get this lying bitch out of here!" yelled a woman in the front row, standing up and waving her fist. But from the back of the room, someone else yelled back, "Let her speak!"

Felicity stammered, "But you've always been a backer of Pat Farnsworth. How..."

Jen quickly cut in.

"I *was* a backer of hers, but that's because, like most of the people in journalism, my mind was closed to ideas that didn't mesh with the belief that more government is always the solution. Luckily, some good folks I met in Laguna Beach opened my eyes to what's really happening to the country. I realized that I had been manipulated by mind-numbing slogans that obscured the truth, which is that some Americans like to control and exploit others. As a journalist, I admit that I've been at fault for selling the people a terrible bill of goods.

"My other book goes into a lot of detail on the damage Pat Farnsworth and other big government fanatics have done to America, and what it will take for us to get out of our tailspin. I hope you'll download and read it, Felicity."

Felicity shot a glance at Wes Abramowicz, who shrugged and made a hand gesture for her to continue the show.

"Well, that's quite astounding, Jen. You say that some people triggered your change of mind?"

"That's right Felicity."

"What happened is that I was assaulted by two criminals who meant to harm me and they were stopped by a man with a gun, an *illegal* gun. A gun he wouldn't have had if he had obeyed the former president's directive on firearms. Afterward, I was willing to listen to him, a Black man who loves America and hates what's happening to it. I also listened to neighbors of his who got me thinking—actually *thinking*—for the first time in many years."

Felicity looked panic-stricken. The shouting from the audience was growing louder. Two women were swinging their purses at each other. More were standing up and surging toward the stage.

"That's very interesting, " she stammered. "And now we have to go to a commercial break."

For the second time in six months, Jen felt the grip of fear.

Wes Abramowicz ran out on the stage, saying loudly to Felicity and Jen, "This is getting bad. The network says to end this before things get completely out of hand. Follow me."

The three left the stage. As they reached the corridor, Felicity turned to Jen and said with a sneer, "I don't like your ideology."

Jen stopped and looked up into her contorted face.

"I don't care what you think, Felicity, but respecting other people's freedom to live their lives isn't an ideology. It's basic decency."

Wes and Jen then walked quickly down a corridor toward the Exit sign. As they reached the door, Wes looked around furtively. He whispered to Jen, "I've called you a taxi. I must say, that took a lot of guts. But now you're marked—probably more than anyone else in America. *Please* never let them silence you."

"Thank you, Mr. Abramowicz. I won't."

Jen stepped out into the cold air, got into the waiting taxi, and thought to herself, *What a way to celebrate Beethoven's birthday*.

On the ride home, Jen checked email on her phone. Scrolling down, she found the one she was expecting—from Will Collier. It read, "I posted your book on our site last night, then contacted all those people you said would be interested in it. So far, it has been downloaded over fifteen thousand times and that show this morning will no doubt raise the number exponentially. Good job!"

At the same time, *Vista del Oceano* became a hive of activity.

Pat Farnsworth was sleeping off a severe hangover when her phone rang. She blinked at the screen several times before seeing that Courtney Oliver was calling.

"Why the fuck are you calling me at this hour, Courtney?!" she hissed into her phone.

"Madam President, I'm very sorry to wake you up, but something has happened with the launch of your biography."

Sitting up in bed, Pat yelled into her phone, "Well, what is it?"

Oliver swallowed hard.

"Um, Jennifer Van Arsdale was on TV this morning to begin the publicity campaign for the book. I'm afraid that she, um, caused something of a riot when she said that besides your biography, she also wrote a second book she called the *antidote* for it. She also blamed you for an array of national problems and said that she thinks you were America's worst president."

"What!" yelled Pat. "You mean to say that the little bitch turned into a rat? She must have been bought off by some right-wing plutocrats. And what the hell do you mean, an *antidote book*?"

"Well, Madam President, apparently while she was out here back in May, there was an incident that brought her into contact with some people in Laguna Beach who," Oliver paused to choose his words carefully, "who do not like you. Somehow, they convinced her that you were not our greatest president, but," again he paused, "but the worst."

"Dammit, Courtney, we have to get that money back and we have to stop this goddam 'antidote' book of hers!" Pat roared.

"And find out who these disloyal people are and what we can do to them!"

Oliver took a moment to dab away some beads of sweat from his forehead.

"As to the first thing, Madam President," Oliver said quietly, "she did fulfill her contract and wrote a book that we approved. I'm sorry to say it, but all that money is gone. As to the second, we don't control the internet. We can't stop people from downloading her book. And by now, it's probably so widely dispersed that there's nothing we can do."

"Never tell me there's nothing we can do, Courtney," bellowed Pat. He then heard the sound of breaking glass. The line went dead.

When Jen got home, Allegro was waiting at the door. She scooped her up, then went to the kitchen table and opened her laptop. She found that dozens more emails had accumulated. One that she was certain would be there indeed was—from Gabrielle Tartakover. It read, "Your conduct has disgraced the *Washington Post*. Clear out anything of yours from the office. You are hereby terminated."

Jen hit reply and wrote, "I don't care to be associated with you any longer, so that's fine with me." She hit send.

Another email was from Alexander Oistrakh. It read, "Dear Jen, Thanks for sending me your antidote book. I started it last night and it is superb. If you find yourself in legal trouble over this, as I suspect you will, I will see what I can do to help you. Best regards, Alex."

Jen wrote back, "Dear Alex, You did so much to help me understand the world. I read everything you suggested and much more. I appreciate your offer to help and I'll let you know if I need it. Jen"

Her phone rang—it was Maddy.

"Hi, Maddy."

"Wow, sis!" said Maddy. "Your appearance on Felicity's show caused quite an uproar. TV stations are replaying it and talk radio hosts are talking about it. I'm sure you'll be hearing from some of them."

"No doubt you're right, Maddy," Jen answered, "but I'm not sure I want to do more media just now. I'm pretty tired."

A text came in from Samantha Swan: "Sorry we ever dined together, Jen. How could you do such a horrid thing? I hope they throw you in prison forever."

No sense in replying to that.

Jen decided she needed some rest and flopped down on her sofa, Allegro curled up beside her.

Two hours later, she was awakened by loud noises outside. Going to the window, she peeked through the blinds and saw that a large crowd had gathered outside her townhouse.

They kept shouting, "Jen Van Arsdale is a disgrace. We demand she leave this place!"

Stones bounced off the window. At least the money she had spent on security against criminals was proving its worth. The new windows were unbreakable.

Jen crept upstairs to get what she figured would be a safer look at the crowd that was now only a few feet from her thankfully reinforced door. She decided to take some video with her phone, and just as she started recording, a news truck rolled up. A young reporter and cameraman got out.

Once they had set up, Jen could hear the reporter say, "We are in front of the townhouse of *Washington Post* writer Jennifer Van Arsdale, who earlier today caused a furor with her appearance on the *Today with Felicity* show, where she was supposed to discuss her new biography of former president Pat Farnsworth.

"But instead of talking about the biography, Ms. Van Arsdale said that she has written a second book that sharply criticizes the former president and her policies. That led to a commotion in the studio. Ms. Van Arsdale fled that scene to cower here in her townhouse. But protesters learned her address and have turned out in large numbers to let their feelings be known."

The reporter turned to a middle-aged woman wearing a gray coat and stocking cap. "Ma'am, could you tell viewers why you are here?"

"Yeah. It's because the woman who lives here is a louse. She's one of those right-wing funded moles who want to turn the clock back. But we won't stand for it! We have to make an example of her!"

The crowd cheered.

A police car drove by, slowing down as it passed the mob of protesters, then continuing down the street.

The reporter turned to a young man in a gray hoodie.

"Sir, what do you think about what Jennifer Van Arsdale has done?"

He took a piece of paper from his pocket and read, "I'm here to peacefully protest. We can't tolerate writers spewing out hateful falsehoods about a great leader like Pat Farnsworth."

He put the paper back in his pocket and took out an egg-sized stone, which he threw against the door.

Jen had enough video and sent it to Maddy.

Maddy quickly texted her back, "I don't think they will give you any peace. Can you sneak out the back where I'll pick you up?"

"Good idea," Jen texted back. "I'll watch for you. Let me know where you're in the alley."

Half an hour later, Jen's phone rang. It was Maddy. "I'm just pulling behind your building, Jen."

Through the blinds, Jen could see her sister's dark red Subaru. She picked up Allegro and went out, making certain to lock the door, then hurried to get into Maddy's car. Bonnie was in the back, asleep in her car seat.

"Now let's hope we can get out of here without being seen," said Maddy.

They held their breath until Maddy had driven a block, leaving the protest behind. For a minute, both were quiet. Then Jen spoke up.

"You know, Maddy, I understand what that's all about. For years, I have been writing things that sent readers the message that anyone who opposed progressivism—what you call statism—were evil, contemptible humans who should never be listened to, but instead treated as though they were from some hostile, inferior tribe. Now that I have had a change of mind, I'm getting that same treatment. Of course, I never advocated intimidation and violence, but I defended the people who engaged in them. Journalism has a lot to answer for. *I have a lot to answer for.*"

"You're right, Jen," said Maddy, "but at least you were willing to say something. How many other journalists have ever admitted that they were wrong?"

"I can't think of a single one," answered Jen.

When they got to Maddy's home in Alexandria, Bonnie woke up. "Aunt Jen," she squealed.

"Hi, Bonnie! How's my big girl?" said Jen.

They walked inside and sat at the kitchen table. Jen put Allegro down and Bonnie started playing with her.

"I just don't think things are safe for you at your house, Jen," said Maddy. "Why don't you stay here for a while?"

"Yeah, Aunt Jen—stay with us," said Bonnie.

"I would love to stay with you," Jen said, "but I'm afraid those protesters will somehow find out I'm here and start protesting just like they did at my home. And besides, I'm sick of Washington. I would like to get away for a while—to sort of disappear. I'm afraid of the mobs and I'm afraid of the government."

Maddy reached over and gently took Jen's hand in hers.

"I completely understand how you're feeling, but you can't actually disappear, Jen. Where would you go? How can you escape detection and being hounded by these disgusting mobs again?"

Jen squeezed Maddy's hand back.

"Actually, I have that figured out, Maddy. One of the great people I got to know in California, a piano teacher named Agnes Mizawa, has said that I can stay with her for as long as I want. I have plenty of cash from ATM withdrawals over the last few weeks—I didn't want much in my account in case the government decides to go after my money."

"That's good, but you don't mean that you have millions in cash, do you, Jen? I know you've been too busy to spend much of that big advance you got."

"No, I only have about twenty thousand, hidden away in my purse," Jen replied, patting it. "The rest I used to buy gold coins from a Mr. Altschuler, another of the people I got to know in Laguna Beach. He said that he'd guard my gold with his life."

"Sounds like a good plan, Jen, but make sure you don't get stopped by the police with that much cash. Have you heard about civil asset forfeiture?"

"Yes, I sure have heard about it and I'll be extremely careful, Maddy. And in fact, civil asset forfeiture was one of the things I learned about from the people in Laguna Beach. It's among the reasons why I now completely get that book you loaned me, *Our Enemy, the State*."

"Okay, so how do you plan to get out there?"

Jen sat back and looked up at the ceiling, then back at Maddy.

"Well, that's a small problem. If I rent a car, that leaves a trace and I'd rather not do that. Could I possibly borrow your Subaru?"

Maddy turned to Bonnie and said, "Bonnie, do you think Mommy should lend her car to Aunt Jen for a while?"

"Yes, I think you should, Mommy," came her answer.

"Josh and I really don't need a second car much anymore. We can easily make do without mine for a while. But are you sure you even remember how to drive, Jen? You haven't owned a car in years."

"Yes, *I can still drive*, Maddy. But I promise to be extra, extra careful with your car."

"What about clothes, Jen? Suppose that this evening we sneak back into your townhouse so you can pack what you need?"

Jen nodded in agreement.

The next morning, Jen left Maddy's house at 6:30 a.m. The people were still asleep, but Allegro purred at Jen as she was getting her things together. She picked her up for a moment and said, "I'll be back as soon as it's safe, Allegro. I promise."

When she got into Maddy's car, Jen found a post-it note stuck on the steering wheel. In Maddy's bold writing, it read: "When you get down to North Carolina, there's a classical, voluntarily funded radio station you'll enjoy—WCPE at 89.7. Drive safe, Jen. Love you."

Jen put the note on the passenger's seat and started the car. She was soon heading south on I-95 in unexpectedly light traffic.

At the Fredericksburg exit, Jen decided to turn on the radio. She heard the announcer say, "In local news, protests resumed this morning at the home of author Jennifer Van

Arsdale, who yesterday shocked the country by denouncing her own biography of former president Pat Farnsworth on live TV. She claimed that Farnsworth was our worst president rather than one of the greatest. Mayor Tidbury said that even though residents in the area complained about the noise, he would not stop the protests at her townhouse since the Constitution protects our right to peaceably assemble and present grievances. And now, the weather..."

Jen turned the radio off. Music was what she needed.

Scrolling through Maddy's playlist, she selected Bach's Third Orchestral Suite and listened to it as she drove south. She concentrated on the music, which helped her put the last twenty-four hours out of her mind.

South of Petersburg, Jen exited for I-85, which would run into I-40 in North Carolina. I-40 would then take her most of the way to the Pacific Coast. She relaxed and enjoyed the drive.

Shortly after crossing into North Carolina, Jen decided that it was time for a break and some hot coffee. She took an exit where there was a Wendy's. She had always liked Wendy's growing up and was sure she could get a good cup of coffee there.

After getting her coffee, Jen sat in a booth. She sipped the hot liquid, watching people come and go, and wondering what she had gotten herself into. Jen spent ten minutes in contemplation, then put the lid on the remaining half of her coffee and went back to the Subaru.

Upon starting the car, Jen noticed Maddy's note. She turned the radio to 89.7 and heard the announcer, a woman, say in a soft and pleasing British accent, "That was *El Catedral* by Paraguayan composer Agustin Barrios. Our next work will be *Finlandia* by Jean Sibelius. Most people know this magnificent piece as a purely orchestral work, but we are going to hear the version Sibelius prepared with chorus, which sings about the longing of the Finns for a free homeland. With the chorus, I believe you'll agree, this great composition is even more stirring."

"And how perfectly fitting this is," thought Jen as the opening chords of *Finlandia* sounded.

A few hours later, near Hickory, North Carolina, Jen pulled off I-40 to refill the car. In the station's shop, she noticed some caps for sale and decided to buy a camouflage hunter's cap.

"With my sunglasses and this cap, nobody could possibly recognize me now," she thought.

By mid-afternoon, in Tennessee, Jen was feeling hungry and saw a sign for a restaurant she had not been in for at least thirty years—Applebee's. She remembered enjoying flavorful salads in Applebee's restaurants when she was a teenager and was glad to find that they were still just as good.

While enjoying her meal, a young mixed-race couple came in with a baby. Even though the baby was loud, no one paid the couple any attention. Jen had long assumed that people in "red states" were hate-filled bigots who'd show their distaste for a mixed family, but there wasn't any evidence of that here. A thought occurred to her. Maybe the hatred ran the other way—from highly educated urban elitists toward the presumably ignorant people who lived out here in the middle of the country.

Jen finished eating, paid her check, then drove on.

Just east of Memphis, Jen was starting to feel tired, so she got off the highway and made for the "Courtyard by Marriott" sign she could see. She paid cash for the room. Once in it, she double-locked the door, closed the curtains, and promptly went to sleep.

The next morning, Jen used the fitness center before anyone else, grabbed some breakfast, then got back on the highway, heading west. She drove across Arkansas and Oklahoma.

When she needed to fill up at a big truck stop near Oklahoma City, a tall, leathery truck driver in a cowboy hat held the door open for her to go in and pay, smiling at her and saying, "After you, ma'am." Jen wondered why so many of her former friends always expressed disdain for the people here in "flyover country." They didn't *know* any of these people yet felt the need to belittle them.

For the first time in decades, Jen was enjoying America.

The headline of the local newspaper on sale caught her eye: Natural Gas Shortage Threatens State as Cold Wave Bears Down. Why was there a natural gas shortage here, she wondered. It took only a few seconds to figure out the answer. Continuing Pat Farnsworth's green agenda, President Barlow had ordered that gas pipelines be shut down to save the planet. Many people in Oklahoma were going to shiver as a result.

More eggs were being broken.

Jen drove on. She spent the night in Tucumcari, New Mexico at a Fairfield Inn. Another day's drive and she'd reach the coast.

The next day, near Holbrook, Arizona, Jen was happily driving along to the exuberant strains of Enescu's First Rumanian Rhapsody when she saw flashing blue lights in her rearview mirror.

Government authorities couldn't know where I am, she thought. And even if they did, I haven't done anything illegal—or have *I*? Then she remembered about civil asset forfeiture. Was her cash well enough hidden away if she were pulled over?

She also grimly thought about what Professor Oistrakh had told her about Lavrenti Beria, vague laws, and the ability to "get" anyone. Jen understood what it was like to live in fear of your government.

Jen felt her pulse racing as the blue lights rapidly approached behind her—and then the police car raced on by. Her heart was pounding, but she and her money were safe—for now, anyway.

It was nearly dark when Jen crossed into California. She needed to stop for gas and decided to call Agnes.

"Hello, Agnes. It's Jen. I think I'll be at your house in a few hours, depending on traffic."

"Oh, I'm so glad to hear your voice, Jen," said Agnes. "I'll be up and waiting for you. Drive safely my friend."

CHAPTER 12

Back to the Beach

Jen woke up with the morning light and wondered where she was. In a moment, she remembered that she was in Agnes Mizawa's guest room. She dressed and walked toward the kitchen. The smell of fresh coffee greeted her.

Agnes was seated at the table.

"Good morning, Jen. I'm happy to see that you're also an early riser. Would you care for some coffee?"

"Oh, yes please, Agnes. It smells divine."

Agnes poured Jen a cup and handed it to her.

"Have you been following the news since you left Washington?"

"No, I haven't Agnes. I needed a break from the world. Driving out here was just me, music, and scenery."

Agnes took a long breath.

"Well, Jen, the country has been talking about you all week.

"Of course, the newspapers have excoriated you. The *New York Times* said that you viciously blindsided President Farnsworth with your unauthorized book and that the Hate Speech Commission must scrutinize it for violations of the law. The *San Francisco Chronicle* called you 'deeply irresponsible' and 'an embarrassment to the profession of journalism.' Your old friends at the *Washington Post* attacked you for acting in bad faith and writing your second book that 'no doubt is filled with falsehoods and misinformation.'"

Jen chuckled at that. Agnes sipped her coffee and continued.

"President Barlow thought your escapade so important that she gave a national address on it, saying that it 'proved the need to finally bring the internet under comprehensive federal regulation.' Congressional leaders have promised to fast-track new legislation to crack down on seditious writings that undermine confidence in the government.

"In the media world, you are Public Enemy Number One. Felicity Mantilla devoted an entire program to you, with a supposedly balanced discussion—two women who agreed that your bad book had to be suppressed and a third whose only disagreement with them was that they didn't go far enough. She wants you placed under arrest until you apologize to the nation and admit that you were paid by right-wing billionaires to pull your stunt."

Jen sipped her coffee and nodded slowly as Agnes recounted all the anger she had stirred up.

"Facebook is blocking any posts that mention your 'antidote' book. On Google, searches for your name bring up all your old writings and your biography of Pat Farnsworth, but nothing about your criticism of her or anyone who backs you. People I know who use Twitter tell me that anything favorable about you is blocked, but anything hostile may be posted.

"And I'm sorry to report that the Free People website has been taken down. Google said that we were no longer in compliance with its so-called standards. What that means, of course, is that if you allow criticism of the government, you must be silenced. We're looking for alternatives—while there still are any."

Jen got up to get more coffee and said, "Those big tech people are pretty hostile to the freedoms that allowed them to succeed. Now they're happy to be servants to the ruling elite."

Agnes nodded.

"I'm sure you won't be surprised to hear that college campuses have reacted to your criticism of Farnsworth, Jen. At Oberlin College, students staged a book burning. They printed out several hundred copies of the antidote book as well as copies of works you cited in it, and set them on fire to chants that you were a disgrace to the school. The college's president, Winifred Dennison-Jones, issued a statement saying that the school was revoking your degree and that you were never to set foot on the campus because that would make students feel unsafe."

Jen laughed.

"Without my college degree, I guess I'm officially unemployable."

"You're probably right, Jen."

"Up at Stanford, your friend Professor Oistrakh sent out an email in which he praised your antidote book and said that the hysteria over criticism of the government's excessive power showed how far we have regressed from a liberal, tolerant society. Within an hour of that email, a petition was circulating, demanding that the university revoke all his benefits and ban him from the university. Yesterday, Stanford's president announced his decision that Oistrakh will be terminated and banned."

Jen's mouth fell open.

"They did that to an elderly emeritus professor who's battling cancer?"

"Of course they did. He proved himself to be an opponent of progressive ideology. There's no mercy for anyone like that."

Jen stared at the table and said, "I hope I can still contact him."

"On the other hand, Jen, you have gotten a lot of support."

"An editorial in the *Wall Street Journal* said that you have done more to refute the myths that support the country's extremely bloated and increasingly authoritarian government than anyone since H. L. Mencken. They wrote that you'd win a Pulitzer Prize if that still meant anything.

"Also, talk radio has been singing your praises. Antonio Oliviera, who has the biggest following since Rush Limbaugh, said that you are America's Sir Thomas More. Many philosophers and economists who don't fear losing their jobs have praised your book. An economist at the University of Chicago called it 'a devastating rebuttal to the fog of disinformation that shrouds the country.' Discussion groups have sprouted up to talk about the ideas you've presented. Websites are crackling with comments by parents who downloaded your book for themselves and their children. They all agree that it counteracts much of what kids are taught starting in grade school to make them obedient supporters of big government.

"And what the *L.A. Times* sneeringly calls 'the subversive underground'—that would include us—has been spreading your good book all around the world. I have heard that people are working on translations in a dozen languages. It turns out that vast numbers of people want to read your skewering of the conventional wisdom about Pat Farnsworth's greatness and the need for the nanny state.

"You really hit a nerve, Jen. Lots of Americans are saying that they think the government has you under secret arrest, even though Attorney General Mitchell Palmer has denied that."

Jen stared out the window.

"Sir Thomas More, huh? I suppose that means there are people calling for my head."

Agnes set down her coffee cup and looked straight at Jen.

"Some probably would, but what they really want is to discredit you and intimidate others from following your lead in arguing that the government is the obstacle to prosperity and social harmony.

"One more thing that will interest you, Jen, is that your biography of Farnsworth is also selling very well. I'd guess that Farnsworth and the publisher will find some way to weasel out of paying your royalties, but it seems that lots of Americans are reading both of your books and making up their minds. That might help explain why President Barlow's polling numbers have fallen off a cliff."

Jen and Agnes enjoyed a relaxing day, talking about music, walking along the beach, enjoying an ice cream cone from one of the remaining shops in town. Jen noticed that in the six months since she had been there last, Laguna Beach had further deteriorated. A Federal Food Store had taken over what had formerly been a Safeway. It looked dingy.

"The prices are low and the quality is lower," said Agnes, pointing to the store.

"I wouldn't even buy canned vegetables there. I'm worried that eventually we won't have any alternatives."

After walking for a while, Jen realized that it was the twentieth of December, yet hardly any holiday décor was to be seen in town. She commented to Agnes about that.

"You're right, Jen. You won't find much festive spirit in California these days, except for the enclaves of the rich and famous."

Early in the afternoon, Agnes said, "I thought I'd cook up a salmon dinner and invite Will to join us—sound good?"

"It sure does, Agnes."

Will arrived right at six. He was carrying a package under his arm.

"Jen, I'm so happy to see you again. I've got to say that the plan you dreamed up of posting your book on our website and drawing attention to it worked to perfection. Everyone is interested in reading the book that caused so much consternation in official circles. Great work."

"Thanks, Will. But you and Agnes and many of the Free People members also helped by suggesting things I needed to read and places we should notify about the book's availability. I couldn't have done it alone. This was a great team effort."

Will regarded Jen for a moment.

"Yes, it was. No one but you took any risk, however. No one else made any sacrifice. No one else deserves a place in history."

Will cleared his throat.

"Now, there's something else I think I should tell you—unless you've already heard."

"What is it?" Jen asked apprehensively.

"News reports say that you are wanted by the Hate Speech Commission. Chairman Victor Mortain has issued a summons, demanding that you present yourself to face questioning about your anti-Farnsworth book. Not surprisingly, they claim that it contains hate speech. You're expected to appear before the Commission by January fifteen.

"What are you going to do?"

"Well, I had assumed that the government would come after me, but I don't know what I should do. I guess I need a lawyer. I'll call Professor Alex Oistrakh at Stanford if I can get hold of him. Agnes told me earlier today that he has been banished from Stanford for an email that praised my antidote book. I'm certainly not inclined to grovel before the Commission. It makes up its own rules, so who knows what would happen if I put myself in their clutches."

"You're welcome to stay with me as long as you want, Jen," said Agnes.

"If you want to remain safe, I think my home is a pretty good spot. In your hunting cap and sunglasses, you're almost impossible to recognize."

Will shook his head.

"That's true, but I suspect the feds will start nosing around Laguna Beach if you disregard the Commission's summons. After all, you did mention us on Felicity's show. If the government really wants to find you, this probably isn't a safe place.

Depending on what the professor says, you might want to go *really* low and I could help with that."

"Thanks, Will. I will let you know. And what's that under your arm?"

"It's something for you."

He unwrapped a painting and handed it to her.

"That first night in the restaurant, I mentioned that I was getting into painting and over the last several months, I think I have improved a lot. This is a scene up near Monterey where Veronica and I used to love to sit and watch the ocean, the seals, the otters, the birds. I drove up there in June to capture the scene."

Capture it, Will certainly had. The painting was exquisite, enchanting. Jen stared at it for a minute.

"Thank you so much, Will," said Jen in a choking voice.

Jen held the painting for Agnes to see.

"This is so beautiful, Will," she said. "Our magnificent coast—just about the only thing the state can't ruin."

ABOUT THE AUTHOR

George C. Leef is a law school grad who chose to go into college teaching, where he saw how dysfunctional the American education system has become. Later, he became research director for a think tank that focuses on the waste and follies of higher education. He has written on many public policy topics for the *Wall Street Journal*, *Forbes*, and numerous other publications. His previous book covered the Right to Work movement. *The Awakening of Jennifer Van Arsdale* is his first novel.

At every opportunity, Leef extols the virtues of liberty and condemns the harm done by bloated, wasteful, authoritarian government. Through his writing and speaking, he tries to persuade people that a truly liberal society—that is, one based on individual liberty and responsibility—is the only way to enjoy prosperity, harmony, and progress. He and his wife, Ann, live in Raleigh, NC.

CPSIA information can be obtained
at www.ICGtesting.com
Printed in the USA
LVHW080810310522
720098LV00015B/713

9 781637 583562